M O D E R N   G R

ASTK

CW00826078

EUGENIA FAKINOU

Astradeni

Translation
H. E. CRITON

KEDROS

Typeset in Greece
by Photokyttaro Ltd
219, Imitou Str., Athens
and printed by
H & G. Zaharopoulos & D. Sitaras
Moskato, Athens
For
Kedros Publishers, S.A.
3, G. Gennadiou Str., Athens 106 78
Tel. 36.09.712 — Fax 36.31.981
June 1991

Cover design by
Dimitris Kalokyris

ISBN 960-04-0483-6

This morning I got up, washed my face, got dressed, said my prayers, and drank my tea. Then I went out into the yard and sat on the low wall. The stone was still damp from the night dew. But nobody said, "Move along, you'll get a tummy-ache." Everybody's running to and fro like mad, like the time we lost our Little Manoli.

Our Little Manoli was thirteen. He hadn't been ill. When he came home from school that day he said he had a tummy-ache. He didn't want to eat anything, though we had his favourite dish for dinner: potatoes in tomato sauce and fish. Mother yelled at him for having eaten unripe pears.

"I have not!" he kept saying and wouldn't stop throwing up. Then they called the doctor. The island's been without a doctor ten months now. We make do, as Mother says, with the army doctor. Since he's doing his military service and has no say in the matter, he's stationed on our island. He's here to take care of the soldiers but he takes care of us people too when necessary. He pressed Little Manoli's tummy with his fingers and said:

"To Rhodes with him at once! He's got appendicitis; he must have an operation. You must hurry!"

Fotaras spoke on the phone for ages. Two hours later the helicopter came. It took away Little Manoli and my parents. I stayed with Auntie Thareini for ten days. Then Father and Mother came back on the boat. They were too late for Little Manoli, for that thing wrong with his tummy. Now, as Mother says, he's resting in the Holy Trinity churchyard. I've planted carnations there, because he liked them. There's an oil lamp too, which Mother and I light every evening. Next summer I'm going to carry fine white sea pebbles to Little Manoli's place to make it look pretty. But that's nonsense, because I'm not going to be here next summer. I'm leaving today. *We're* leaving, that is, Mother, Father and me. We're going to the big city, to Athens.

I'm wearing my good shoes, the patent leather ones with the bows; and my red jacket with the yellow ducklings; and white socks. You don't go to Athens every day, after all. You must be all dressed up when you go. There the ladies are always pretty and all dressed up. I've seen them on Auntie Thareini's TV. It's not her TV really; it belongs to her son Yanni who was in Australia. He brought it from there. Yanni is the handsomest cousin I have. His father Sotiri is handsome too, even though he's sixty. The foreign ladies, the tourists, call him Anthony Quinn, which is to say, "You're very good-looking." One of them kept offering him cigarettes, saying, "Zorba, Zorba, Zorba," which means "have some cigarettes." He took the cigarettes and went off with her to show her how he makes butter.

Uncle Sotiri has sheep and goats. Auntie Thareini, who married him, is my mother's sister. "He's a good man," she says, "he's never raised a hand against me. I bore him six children, but it's the livestock that's been my undoing."

There isn't much grass on the island; it's all rocks.

8

That's why they take the flocks to a place called Hames, one-and-a-half hour's climb up the mountain. They start out at four in the morning and come back in the afternoon. Well, what d'you expect, Auntie's worn herself out. And it wasn't as if her mother, my grandma Eleni, hadn't warned her, "Heed my words, child, don't marry a shepherd."

She knew alright; she'd married a shepherd herself, Grandpa Sotiri. Her mother, Great-Grandma Martha, kept warning her too, but she was beyond salvation! Grandpa sang under her window, so she married him. They had seven children, my mother being one of them. Well, my cousin Yanni has dark eyes, dark hair, and a black moustache. He looks just like the man on the BRAVO coffee packet. He left the island and went to Australia. He can tell you great stories about it; and the people there speak English.

"What's the idea, you sitting there like a clod?" That's my mother yelling. She gives me the shoulder bag with the water bottle and the meatballs to carry. Father goes first with our two suitcases. The good one is the wooden one with our clothes in it. The other, the chequered cloth one, we borrowed from Maria. We'll send it back empty after we've unpacked our linen. Mother is carrying two calico shopping bags that she's made herself. They're full of jars of honey, cheese and whole-wheat rusks to keep us going during the first days in the big town. They're for gifts as well. You can't go empty-handed. There are many of our islanders living in Athens and Piraeus. But *we're* to live in Athens.

The bag with all the food and water is heavy and cuts into my shoulder, but I daren't say a word. I'm afraid they may box my ears, they're that irritable both of them. God knows why, for, after all, we're going to Athens. So I switch shoulders every so often. I go down ten steps with the bag over my right shoulder and then change over to the left; ten steps with the bag over the left shoulder, then change again. The women of our neighbourhood have come out with their censers to see us off. In the censers they're burning small bunches of dried palm leaves from Palm Sunday. Anna is weeping and makes the sign of the cross over us, "Godspeed and good luck to you!" What do we need luck for? It's Athens we're going to after all. Sotiria, Anna's daughter, looks askance. She's jealous, I can feel it. I'm off to Athens, and she hasn't even been to Rhodes. And what's Rhodes after all, just two hours by boat. Of course, her brother lives in Canada. He sends her those funny long dresses. What rubbish! And it isn't as if he had some kind of decent job, her brother. A dishwasher, that's what he is; with long working hours too. Well, *my* father's going to Athens so he won't have to wash dishes, so there!

As long as Father had the caique he was doing fine. Our caique was the most beautiful fishing boat on the island, broad and sitting well in the water. We had painted her bright red all over. The harbour master kept saying to Father, "Change the colour, you're asking for trouble!" Father turned a deaf ear. Why should he listen? He liked her this way. After all, can't you paint your boat even whatever colour you fancy? Along her sides we had painted three stripes, a yellow, a blue, and a white one. On her bows we had also painted two blue eyes. And she was named SEAGIRL, after me. Because I was a born seagirl, Father said.

When there was no school, you didn't have to look far for me; I was bound to be on board. I drew water with a pail and washed the deck. You need the right technique for that. You need to give the pail that extra little jerk at the right moment, so that it won't hit the gunwale and scratch the wood, yes sir! Later Father took me along when he sailed out. Our Little Manoli was still with us then, and he taught me a trick. He taught me many tricks of course, but, well, that one really impressed me. You washed a cucumber in the sea and then kept dipping it into the seawater after every bite to make it taste salty. The same trick worked with tomatoes.

Our caique was properly fitted out for fishing, but we no longer used it as a fishing boat. "Fish has grown scarce," Father had said with bitterness in his voice. Petrol prices had risen too. Besides they'd put that rubbish on the market, the deep-frozen stuff; but it was cheap and people bought it. Father gave the matter some thought and turned our boat into a greengrocer's.

We sailed to Cos, loaded tomatoes, marrows, watermelons, cucumbers, sweet melons. We had our own secret source of supply at Mastichari which is round the back of Cos as we face it. It was a lot of trouble, of course, and a long way by sea, but Father preferred Mastichari. We loaded the boat to the gills. It took hours, the weighing and the loading, with Manoli and me both helping. We spent the night at Mastichari. Old Theodore, who owned the vegetable garden, gave us dinner. And quite a sight they were, those sweet melons and watermelons growing in the sand a few feet away from the sea. You wouldn't believe how sweet those watermelons tasted.

Next morning, at dawn, we crossed over to Calymnos. We sold some of the goods and went on to the small island of Pserimos. There we didn't sell much. No people lived there, only some fishermen. But Father said Old Theodore grew his watermelons for everybody. We lit a fire with the fishermen and made fish soup, or grilled fish for dinner. We left after dark to round Cape Crios before the meltemi wind rose. We touched Nisyros and Tilos, then made straight for Panormitis and sailed back home. There we sold out at last. We cleaned the boat, stayed home a couple of days to tidy up, and back to Mastichari. It was a good life, but the helicopter and the Rhodes hospital cost us our caique, all because of our Little Manoli, God rest his soul.

They advised my father to sell our property at Saint

Constantine's. "Not on your life," Father said. "My father, my grandfather, my great-grandfather were all born there. Never, I say!" so he sold the caique.

Forty days after our Little Manoli's death they offered Father a job at the TRATA restaurant. They knew we found it hard to make ends meet. My aunts and uncles were helping discreetly, but Father was a proud man.

"Go to the TRATA, Nicola," my mother said. He glared at her, he bristled.

"Me a slave waiting on lords and their ladies? No, thank you."

"How about helping out in the kitchen then?" Mother ventured.

The TRATA was the island's only restaurant. It was a gold mine. It served deep-frozen snapper for fresh, Pacific octopus as the local product. The tourists raved. There were fish nets laid out in front to make believe they had just been drawn in and were drying in the sun. Father at the TRATA would have been like a lion in a cage.

"No," he said, "I'm going to Athens."

13

We've got to Myloi which is a flat bit. Auntie Thareini and Uncle Sotiri are waiting for us. My uncle takes the chequered suitcase to relieve Father. We go on down. Mother and Auntie seem to have a lot to say to each other. They're talking about Little Manoli's oil lamp, for sure. Last night we took three kilos of oil over to Auntie's, so she can keep the lamp going. We took her a little bag of incense too, the smuggled kind with musk in it. We've got lots of smuggled goods on the island that the Turks bring across. After all, our distance from Turkey is the time it takes to smoke a cigarette, as they say. We've always had good dealings with the Turkish fishermen. On our island there's no livestock other than sheep and goats. The pigs don't count. Each household raises one for Christmas only. Well, in the evening the butchers' hooks are empty; in the morning beef is hanging everywhere. Where does all this beef come from overnight? From Turkey, of course. We, in turn, barter detergents. Our island buys the largest amounts of ROL and TIDE in all of Greece; so much, that is, that a gentleman from ROL came to see what we do with all that detergent. What are we to say, that we barter with the Turks?

We've reached the school, my school. School's out, but our teacher, Mrs. Antigone, is standing at the door. I wonder what for. I hope she doesn't start with the usual,

14

"Do your homework, watch your decimals and Religious Instruction."

Mrs. Antigone is a stranger; she wasn't born on our island, that is. The Ministry posted her here ten years ago. I have it from Maria's mother who ought to know. She was very young, our island seemed sweet and so did Michalio, so she married him.

"Pity, the schoolteacher's buried herself alive here," was said at the time.

"It's no match, a schoolteacher and a carpenter; it won't work," they said.

Yet our teacher's fine, with pink cheeks, always smiling, and she's got three children, one still at the breast. So I say a schoolteacher and a carpenter are a good match, provided the schoolteacher likes children and the carpenter his wood.

Mrs. Antigone shakes hands with Father and Mother. This is a bad sign, because on the island we greet each other with words or kisses; handshakes are a foreign thing. Now she's standing in front of me. I know it, because I keep my eyes lowered and I'm looking at her shoes. They're brown, flat and dusty. And her feet are broad, standing firmly on the flagstones.

"Astradeni, look at me."

Her eyes are green like olive oil with little black specks in them. Her nostrils are a bit wide. Her lips are smiling. Her eyes are telling me something; I don't quite understand it, I don't get it; it's something that troubles me.

"You're leaving us, Astradeni. Yesterday I gave your father your report, so you can enrol at your new school in Athens. You'll see many new things; keep your eyes open. Above all, don't forget what you've left behind,

And remember how much we love you."

She kisses me on both cheeks. Ma'am kisses me on both cheeks! Is Sotiria watching this, I wonder?

"Yes, Ma'am," I say.

Shall I kiss her hand now? Isn't that the proper thing to do? I look into her eyes and kiss her on both cheeks too. Since I'm never going to see her again, I think I've done right. I can feel it, I can see it; she liked it and is smiling.

We move on and make another stop in front of the café. Yanni, the owner, a neighbour and friend of Father's, says goodbye, and (fancy that!) he's crying. How depressing; and what's he crying for when we're going to Athens?

Father, head down, is now going in the direction of Yalos. As soon as we're past the desalinisation works, we'll arrive at the Clock Tower. There's no desalinisation any more, that is, but the name has stuck.

Those priests had come from all over at the time, and those gentlemen who made speeches about how much water we were going to collect with those plastic sheets they laid out. They said we would be turning seawater into drinking water with the help of the sun, and our island would become known all over the world. The water, well, if you cooled it, it was passable; otherwise, forget it! Now they've removed all the plastic. What's left is the concrete and metal frames. The mayor promises to plant trees in the place. We'll see, or rather, *they'll* see, those who're staying behind. I'm off to Athens!

16

We've arrived at the Clock Tower. It's past one o'clock; the MIAOULIS will appear any minute now coming from Rhodes. I've never been on such a big ship before. Sotiria is beside me, so she must have seen our teacher kissing me. She's jealous, full of envy, I know it.

The MIAOULIS is in sight. Nothing can hold us back any more. Aunts, uncles, cousins are all around us. As if someone's given them a sudden shove, they all fall to kissing us, hugging us, crying. They're sad that they can't go to Athens too.

They throw the cables from the ship now. My cousin Vassili, who goes to secondary school, fastens the cables around the pollards. The engine is purring. Now they're going to lower the gangplank. The gangplank touches ground on the quay but pulls away, as if it doesn't want to stay put. The swell makes the ship go up and down. Father takes leave of our relatives. I exchange kisses with aunts and cousins.

Father steps on the gangplank loaded down with the suitcases and me close behind followed by Mother with her calico bags. We walk down passages and climb stairs. Now I can see the Clock Tower again and the quay and the people, only I'm looking at them from above. They seem different, smaller and shorter. Father goes off to put away the luggage. Leaning on the railing I look at the people standing on the quay. On the very edge are my girl cousins. Beside them stands Auntie Thareini. She's wearing her best dress. Her hair is

17

parted in the middle, the gray strands covered by the dark ones. Next to her Uncle Sotiri and Vassili, the one who goes to secondary school. There's Michalio who works at the power plant and Hamiotissa, the foxy one. But I must admit she's a very pretty girl. Did I say girl, why, she's a married woman now, she married George. She was in love with him and kept sending letters to him on the ships. For her sake George left the sea and opened a bakery. They've got a son too, Michali. Her mother grumbles, "What, one child only? It's a sin, a sin. Hm, those modern ways; we knew of no such ways in our day."

There he is, her little Michali, playing with his "Matsango" cousins. The nickname has stuck. When they were small we used to ask them if they smoked, and they answered smartly, "We smoke MATSANGO fags," so everyone now calls them "the Matsangos". They go everywhere together too. Cousin Sevasti, their mother, is in Canada with her husband. But the climate there is tough. The kids were always sick, and they sent them back. It's been five years since the "Matsangos" have seen their parents. It's always one thing and another: the fare's too high, next year perhaps, next Easter, in the summer, etc. While Athens, well, it's a stone's throw. You just go on board the MIAOULIS and you're back in a jiffy!

There's Irene too, Fotara's wife, all in black as always. She's carrying a black umbrella too. She's lost her husband *and* her son Lefteri, a second cousin of mine. He was only seventeen. He got sunstroke, they said, and fell into the ship's hold at Jiddah where his vessel was moored. He was badly injured. They took him to Athens where there are many doctors. Irene went to Athens too.

18

He was examined by a lot of doctors, but Lefteri's head was permanently damaged. He lived on for a few months and then passed away. It's good she's got Michalio, her other son. He's an operator at the Telephone Company. He was the one on the phone that time arranging for the helicopter to come for our Little Manoli. We've heard he's to become engaged. Let's hope she's a good girl. I can see my cousins Zambetta and Georgia too. They live in Rhodes most of the time. Their father is a municipal gardener; their mother works as a hotel maid. She's got a weak heart, but she's short of some stamps for the national insurance contributions, so she keeps going.

The MIAOULIS blows her whistle. The heavy cables are untied and dropped noisily into the sea splashing everybody. The crowd takes two steps backwards as if Mrs. Antigone back at school had whistled a command. They wave their arms, I wave back. They wave their arms slowly, like the palm fronds at Pedi.

The ship gives off one long and two short hoots and moves away from the quay. The people grow smaller and smaller. Mother's blowing her nose. Father hasn't shown up yet. Irene has already started on her way home. She and her umbrella form a small "o". The ship makes a manoeuvre and turns around. Now I can see Yalos as it's shown on the postcards made for the tourists. The houses seem all of a piece, without yards, without separate rooms, as if they're painted on a huge piece of cardboard.

The ship will now make another turn to leave the outer harbour. Here Father always slowed down the

19

engine, so that we wouldn't capsize. We always sailed straight between the rocks.

The MIAOULIS is too big; she's got to give them a wide berth.

We were approaching Dysalona when they came round to check our tickets. It was our fellow-islander Nikita, Melpo's son. He's a clerk on the MIAOULIS. He sat beside us on the bench. Father offered him a cigarette, and they started talking.

"So you're bound for Piraeus," Nikita said drawing on his cigarette.

"For Athens," I corrected.

"Athens or Piraeus, it's all the same," he said. His face was too sour, I didn't like it.

"And where are you staying?" he asked Father.

"Stavro, Father Elias' son, has a flat in Kypseli," Father said. "He's now sailing on the PALASKA and said we could stay as long as we liked. He'll have left the keys with Michalio, the tailor."

Ha, so it's a flat Stavro's got; and I thought it was a house. I've never lived in a flat. I'll write about it to Sotiria, whose house is under "Preservation Order", to make her green with envy. She envied us even on the island, because we weren't under "Preservation Order". When the Archaeological Service came and declared our island a "historic community" and put most houses under "Preservation Order" there was great hue and cry. For when you're "under preservation", you may not dig up the black pebbles of your courtyard pavement and replace them with terrazzo;

21

nor install aluminium window frames; and the main doors must be wooden with the brass knocker in the shape of a hand to go knock, knock! Neither are you allowed to have an electric doorbell, nor a yellow lantern above the door. Inside, says the Archaeological Service, you can please yourself. But the outside must be left as it is: with the roof tiles, the pediments, the caryatids and the painted wooden window frames.

Yes, but if you don't put a metal railing round your yard and have a shiny aluminium main door, how will the others know that you've got money? Sotiria's balcony was pulled down by the Archaeological Service.

"You must build one just like the old one," her family were told. We teased Sotiria to death. We called her "Under Preservation" and she was fit to burst.

As for us in the upper town, we didn't have anything worth preserving. Neither could we afford to add lanterns and fancy door knobs to our main doors. A toilet was all we'd managed to build, and that with concrete blocks and a synthetic corrugated roof. Before that we used the ruined house next door. Rain or shine, there we went. We'd found a corner that was not visible from the road and we relieved ourselves there. The chickens and the sow cleaned up after us.

Every house has its ruin, a derelict house abandoned by those who've gone to Australia or Canada. Over the years roofs have caved in, doors and windows rotted. All that's left are the walls, and the houses are turned into "ruins."

So it's a flat Stavro's got. Congratulations Stavro! "Is he living there alone?" Nikita asked.

"No, with Dino and Sergo, the sons of Nicola Hadzipetrou," says Father. "But now Dino's away on a tanker and Sergo is in England to train as a fridge mechanic."

"Nicola's sons have turned out well," said Mother, "and Zopighi, his wife, was pure gold. You see, he was always away at sea, either on ships or with his caique. She brought the boys up by herself. Her first-born, Lefteri, got the brunt of it. He went to sea at the age of twelve. He helped the second son, Sotiri, study to be a sea captain. Sotiri went to sea and paid for Dino to become a mechanic. Now it's Dino's turn to help Sergo. Only she didn't live to enjoy the fruits of her labours. She wasted away with the cursed disease," Mother said and was still. I know it hurts her to think of Zopighi. She loved her; they'd been friends since childhood sharing all their secrets.

"Have you got any job prospects?" asked Nikita.

"My *koumbaro** Noufri seems to have something in mind for me," Father said.

---

* *koumbaro,* someone related to a family after having been best man at the wedding of one of its members, or godfather to one of its children.

Nikita got up and went inside. It was just us left sitting on the bench. We were wrapped in our heavy jackets, because it was cold for the middle of March.

"Let's have a bite to eat," Mother said and opened the shoulder bag. My late grandma Eleni had woven it on her own loom. Using a red warp she'd woven thin yellow stripes and dark blue broad ones. I bet this bag too smells of Grandma Eleni!

Whatever Grandma wove bore her special scent, a combination of sage tea and dried grape-must pudding. Strange, as if Grandma drank sage tea all the time and ate dried must pudding. But she made the best must pudding ever!

The must came from our vineyard at Kalyvato, below St Constantine's. She strained it and made must pudding with it. She sprinkled cinnamon and sesame seeds on top. The pale pudding, made with white grape must, we ate fresh. The dark grapes were right for dry must pudding. We left it covered in the sun and it dried till it was like leather. We ate it in the winter when there was no fruit.

Toward the end Grandma had become a teeny-weeny thing. She lived alone in her small house. She could live off one boiled marrow for two days. She was waiting for the Angel to fetch her, proper and peaceful, as if she were expecting one of the family to return from abroad. The steps to her house were high. Even I had to gather momentum in order to climb them. She came down the

24

steps sitting on each one of them, and she climbed them on her knees.

I have a colour photograph of me and Grandma. A foreign tourist lady saw me eating grapes on Grandma's steps once. She said something that sounded like, "Shall I take your picture?"

"With my grandma," I told her. The lady laughed. I took her upstairs, and while Grandma was changing into her best jacket, I offered the lady mastic liqueur and Turkish delight. She must've thought the liqueur was water, seeing it's clear, and she gulped it down all at once — and her eyes popped out!

"Oh!" she said and laughed. Then she ate the Turkish delight and drank a glass of water.

Grandma and I stood with our arms around each other under the grapevine pergola with the long white grapes. Grandma's wearing her fancy jacket, the black one with the tiny flowers, and I have my hair in braids. I don't look too bad, only the shadow of the leaves falls on my face making me look too dark-skinned.

Mother has taken cheese pies and meatballs out of the bag. It was me who'd cut the cheese-pie shapes. Mother had made the mixture with warm water, salt, a little olive oil and flour. She kneaded it for a long time, till it was right. Meanwhile I had broken up the feta cheese into crumbs with a big fork. Then we added the eggs and crushed mint. Using a big glass I cut out rounds of flat dough. Mother put the cheese filling on them and covered them with another round of dough. Then I took the parlour-door key and tsak, tsak pressed the lace finish round the edge of the cheese pie. This way it looks pretty and seals the filling inside.

"We're approaching Marathounda," said Father.

When it was too windy we put the caique to port at Marathounda. Only two or three families live there.

"We'll have rough seas at Batos," Mother said.

Mother's afraid of the sea, just like all the other women on our island. They can't even swim. When they came on board our caique to sail to the Panormitis Fair it was a madhouse. They screamed, teased each other and shouted, "You'll drown us!" to Father.

"Sit still, you devils, you'll capsize the boat," Father shouted back.

It was always the lot of them: Thareini with her daughters, Fotara's Irene, Zopighi with her daughter Pelagia.

Pelagia, a blonde with green eyes, tried to outsmart me. Zambetta was with us too that summer at Kalyvato. The grown-ups were working in the vineyards and we played house under the fig tree, the one that produces the royal figs. We had some broken crockery as dishes and served in them overripe figs that had fallen from the tree. We fed our dolls pretending to be mothers with their babies. I had found a small medicine bottle. I'd washed it thoroughly, put two sprigs of rose geranium in it and used it as a vase. Zambetta was jealous: she wanted the bottle for herself. Pelagia wanted it too. Zambetta said, "Kalyvatos is mine, so the vase is mine too."

"You don't say," I shouted, "Kalyvatos is mine!"

Pelagia grabbed me by the braids — she always took Zambetta's side — I grabbed her by the curls, and we kept at each other's hair without a peep, on the sly, because, if the grown-ups got wind of it, we'd be given a thrashing on top of everything else.

Well, the women in our caique laughed only when the sea was calm. The slightest sea swell made them throw up, and then they were very still. My mother isn't talking now either. We've already left Panormitis behind. Our island is growing smaller and smaller; soon it'll disappear. My mother has started crying.

"It's all right, don't cry; we'll manage," says Father.

She says nothing, just goes on crying. My father loves my mother. When he's talking to her, and there's no one else around, his voice becomes gentle. Nor has he ever struck her. And when he's about to make a decision about something important he always asks her opinion.

Father said we should go inside, so we wouldn't arrive in Athens with a cold.

As soon as we opened the door we were hit by a reek of bad air and food. The place was packed with people. Some were eating, others were lying on the floor or on the benches. An old woman was both lying down and eating.

It stinks something awful in here, but on deck it's too cold. And the weather is growing stormier. We've chosen a place near the door. Every time the door opens it takes two to push it shut. It's growing dark.

We must be approaching Cos. Some people over there are having fun. They're sitting in a circle on their blankets, laughing all the time. They have a little girl in their midst singing.

Everything's paid for, everything's paid for,
everything's paid for, my daddy's got the dough
it takes.

She twists her hips and snaps her fingers. Ha, ha, ha, they all laugh.

Some yoghurt and bread-ring vendors have come in, so we must be in Cos.

"After Patmos the weather will make us dance," says Father, "see that you get some sleep."

It's easier said than done. The light is exactly above us. For some time now I've been wanting to go to the toilet, and now I can't hold out any longer. Father will take me and Mother's coming along too. She takes the shoulder bag along. We go down and down some stairs.

28

The engines are thumping beside us. You daren't touch the metal walls, they're so hot. The stench from the toilets combines with the reek of petrol.

Ah, how I miss you, our own caique SEAGIRL! The wind filled your sail and it went rehrrip! and stretched fit to burst with joy. And Little Manoli and me, wrapped up in our blankets, were watching the stars.

I do my business as fast as I can. The boat is rolling and I'm afraid of stepping into the muck. We go back on deck. An icy wind is whistling. Sea spray hits my face and I feel a bit refreshed.

We go back again to that place they call the lounge. I lie on a bench and try to fall asleep. The boards cut into my back. I wake from time to time and look at my father. He's asleep with his head between his hands leaning on the table. My mother seems to be sleeping sitting up. But is she really asleep?

When I open my eyes again the electric light is no longer blinding me. It's daylight. Father's sipping his coffee and gives me a sip too.

"We're around the back of Syros," he says. "It'll be another six or seven hours."

Mother has opened the shoulder bag again. I can only eat some cheese pie. The meatballs look soggy; they smell bad to me. People are sitting up on their blankets. Their faces look yellow. Nobody seems to feel like eating. The little girl that was dancing last night is sitting down now too.

"Do you want some tea?" Father asks.

"Not clean enough," says Mother. "So many people drinking tea, they won't be washing the cups properly."

"I want some tea, even if the cups aren't clean," I say.

Father brings me a glass of tea. He's fetched it from the boat kitchen. I blow on it, because it's piping hot. Mother shows me how to drink it without touching the rim of the glass. Otherwise I'll be covered with lip sores, she maintains. It's a bother drinking it as she says, but I do it. The tea has warmed me up.

We go on deck. We're sailing past some land. "It's the island of Kea," Father tells me. We're sailing quite close to it; no houses, only a lighthouse. When I grow up I'll marry a lighthouse keeper. We'll be living alone in the small, round lighthouse. A ship will occasionally drop food for us, but we'll also keep chickens and rabbits and grow lettuces on the side. And when the sea is rough my husband and me will be listening to the waves breaking on the rocks. And there'll be a time when my husband will save a ship with a crew of thirty. He'll save them from drowning, that is. And then the Prime Minister himself will come to congratulate him and present him with a Greek flag, as he did with the woman of Ro, the only inhabitant of that tiny island. I'll be wearing our fancy island dress with the fur trimming, and they'll show me on TV. And when I'm old I'll be going to the Rhodes Hospital and have all my medical tests done free of charge, without paying a penny, that is.

Father points at some land saying it's Attica. So it's the end of islands: the moment has come at last. For "What's the capital of Attica?" as Mrs. Antigone used to ask — Athens.

"As soon as we sight Cape Sounion," says Father, "it'll be three hours to Piraeus."

We're sailing quite close to shore now. I can see the cars. There are cars on Rhodes and on Cos, but I've never been in one. I don't like them; I'm afraid of them, but I've never told anyone.

Father shows me the airport and a plane that circles above it. In a little while it lands and rolls like a car in the street and I can no longer see it. Father's been in a plane. It was when he flew to join the crew of a boat in the Persian Gulf. My father is a third engineer. He worked on ships till he made the money to buy the caique. But now he doesn't want to go to sea any more. Where would that leave us? After the loss of our Little Manoli Mother won't hear of his going to sea. That's why we're going to Athens. Father will find a good job and we'll have a good life.

Mother appears in the door and beckons. She takes me to a tap, washes my face and wets my hair. She undoes my braids and combs my hair. Strange, she only does this when we're getting ready for church; on other days I'm left to cope by myself. She straightens my socks and my jacket. Father appears, smiling.

"Come on," he says, "Piraeus is in sight."

I run on deck. Everybody's leaning on the railing watching. Golly, so many houses, and how tall they are! one, two, three, four, five floors!

"Father, the houses are five floors high. And that one there is six! And that tower?"

"That's a grain elevator."

I look at him. I don't understand.

"From that they load grain on the ships," he explains.

There's so much to look at! Tugs whistle beside us. Other ships that are moored, are being loaded. The beacon ahead of us is flashing.

Father takes us back inside. We must find our suitcases and disembark. Mother and me are waiting for him sitting on the bench. Mother crosses herself and moves her lips. I'm awfully anxious; where are we going now? Are we going to have to get into a car? Will we be able to find Stavro's house, his flat I mean? And if he hasn't left the keys behind, what are we going to do?

Father comes with the suitcases. We walk along some passages again. It's crowded and we get stuck. We stand and wait. I'm squeezed in the crush. They'll crease my good jacket. Finally we move on. We're going down the gangplank, I can feel it, but I can't see anything. There are lots of people left and right. I mustn't lose Father and Mother. I grab Mother by the skirt. I step off the gangplank and am standing on firm ground. But the one whose skirt I'm holding on to isn't my mother!

"Mother!" I shout and my voice cracks.

"This way, Astradeni," my mother calls.

We walk beyond a railing and put down our luggage. What a way to disembark, pushed by the crowd all the way! Father looks at us smiling.

"Now," he says, "we must find Michalios, the tailor, in Philhellinon Street." We ask a gentleman where Philhellinon Street is.

"You'll walk along the waterfront," he says, "till you come to the Port Authority. Just beyond, Philhellinon Street begins. Turn left and walk till you come to the number you're looking for."

The gentleman is very good-looking. He's wearing a clean shirt, a tie, a jacket matching his trousers. His shoes are beautifully polished. He's carrying a briefcase with locks on it. He must be very important. We walk along together since he's going to the Port Authority on business. He says he's an agent. Well, I was right in my guess he was important. That's Athens for you. The very first person we meet turns out to be somebody important too.

We get to the Port Authority. The gentleman leaves us. We must cross the street now — easier said than done. Cars are coming from two directions and no gap between them. Neither do they stop at all.

Father says, "When I say NOW, you cross the street with me and fast!" We wait a while, but nothing doing. Cars are passing all the time.

"Watch out; when that blue car has gone past, get ready. Astradeni, you hold on to your mother's skirt. NOW!" says Father and goes off.

Mother starts after him, steps past the blue car but is frightened by the yellow one coming up. She stops. I stop too in the middle of the street. Holy Panormitis, I say to myself shutting my eyes, please perform a miracle, we'll be run over. I hear some screeching noises and a car stopping. Father is in the middle of the road gesticulating to stop the cars. We cross running. A gentleman driving a white car rolls the window down and, making that rude gesture that means damn you, shouts:

"There, peasants! Now go to hell!"

Us, peasants? We're islanders, we're not peasants.

34

But even if we were, what of it? Was he going to run us over? I've never been so frightened in all my life.

No, I take it back. I have been so frightened before: that time at Saint Constantine's.

I was playing beside our little house while the others were working. Then I saw a length of rubber hose on the path among the blades of grass. It was a fine, fat length of rubber hose, just right for stepping on and swaying to and fro. And that's exactly what I did, except that the rubber hose was a snake. It lifted its tail, then its head and bit me. It was a bite in my leg like two pin pricks side by side. I raised the dead with my screams. They killed the snake which was a viper. My mother started crying. They fetched Mercouras at once. Mercouras was better than a doctor and more popular, because he sucked out the viper's poison. I thought I was passing out, breathing my last.

Mercouras took out his bottle of ouzo and a razor blade. With the razor blade he made two cuts. I don't know where, because I turned my head the other way. Then he took two sips of ouzo. He didn't swallow it but swished it around in his mouth. Then he put his mouth on the bite and started sucking. He sucked out the venom with the blood and spat it out. He sipped some ouzo again, and again he sucked. Then they tied my leg with strips torn from a clean napkin. I was in pain for days, but I survived.

We arrive at a chemist's. Next door is a hotel, and next to that is "Vriti", the tailor. His name's actually

Michalios Diamandakis, but "Vriti" is his nickname. On the island you go by your nickname. If someone asks for you using your last name, nobody knows you. Michalios is a small man, so they call him "Vriti", which means chick-pea.

We enter the tailor's shop. There's a counter, and behind the counter Michalios is cutting some piece of material with a big pair of scissors. He's wearing his tape measure around his neck. There's a sewing machine too. When he sees us he drops everything and hugs us.

"Welcome," he says. "Have a seat."

That's easier said than done. What's there to sit down on? The shop is full of suitcases, baskets, bundles. All Symians deposit their orders and their packages here. Michalios is our postman. He arranges which fellow-islander will kindly deliver a box of medicines to someone in Symi. It's him also who'll impose on someone to take the homemade noodles to Sevasti in some faraway Piraeus area, God bless him.

Michalios wants to hear all the news. But what news? He knows everything already: deaths, engagements, weddings, christenings, whether on Symi or in Athens. Father asks for the key.

"I haven't got it," says Michalios. We freeze. There we are. Just as I feared. What's to be done now?

"Stavro's left the key with Maria Tsavari. She lives in the same block on the second floor," says Michalios. Block... second floor... what language is Michalios speaking?

But we needn't worry, he adds, he's going to ring Maria right now. He dials a lot of numbers, then smiles at us while waiting on the phone.

"Hi ya Mai-ree, an' how's yer good self," he says with a loud laugh.

Well, that's really heavy Symian dialect for you! Whatever possessed Michalios to slip back into it, I wonder.

After speaking on the phone with Maria, he told us that she'd be at home expecting us. She was going to give us the key and anything else we needed. Maria Tsavari, daughter of the "Liar". It was the name Maria's father was known by. Not that he was a liar; he was a good soul, but he always promised to come and help with wood chopping or sheep shearing, and he never showed up. He had five daughters; he had too much to look after. Maria's his third. She left the island when she was quite young and went to Egypt. Now she lives in an apartment block in Kypseli, yes sir! And that's where we're going too.

"Listen," Michalios tells Father, "you'll take the underground, the train. I'll tell you how to get to the station. You'll take the train and get off at the stop called Victoria. You'll come up from the underground and take trolley bus number 2 that goes to Kypseli. You'll get off at Kypseli Square. There you ask for Limnos Street, you find number 101 and ring Maria's bell. Unless you take a taxi that will deliver you C.I.F. at Maria's."

"How much will that cost?" asks Father.

"Hm, two hundred's in it for sure. But even by public transport, you need ten drachmas each for the train, that's thirty. And thirty for the trolley, that's sixty; *and* you'll have all the bother. By taxi it'll be easier with all the luggage. Only watch out that the taxi driver doesn't take you for a ride and you have to pay more. I'll write down the address for you, and you tell him to take you

37

via Piraeus Street."

Father took the slip of paper and picked up the suit-cases. We said goodbye to Michalios and left.

My heartbeat grows faster. The moment has come when I'll have to get into a car, there's no way round it.

"Let's find a taxi," Father says, stopping at the corner.

All sorts of cars drive past. On some of them it says TAXI. It must mean they're faster than the rest.* One of these fast ones stops in front of us and the driver asks if we want a taxi. Father says we want to go to Kypseli via Piraeus Street.

"I'll oblige," says the driver getting out of the car. "I'm going to the workshop for repairs, but Kypseli's on my way."

He opened a kind of wide door at the back and piled our luggage in. Father opened a door behind the driver's seat. He pushed Mother and me inside and squeezed in beside us.

"What did you all squeeze into the back like that for?" asked the driver and gave us a straight look. "I trust there's nothing wet and dripping in your bags to stain the upholstery."

Father shook his head, embarrassed. Mother crossed herself trying not to be seen doing so.

The driver put his foot down on something, pushed a metal bar, and the car started. I got the jitters; he's go-ing to drive us over the edge somewhere for sure. Holy Panormitis, he's turning! Another car is turning too

* TAXY is Grrek for "fast".

38

from the other side, and a lorry's coming from the opposite direction. I'll shut my eyes, I can't bear it. But, hey, our car has stopped. Is it for this short ride he wants two hundred drachmas? Why, we should've gone on foot. No, he starts up again.

Well, I'll look at the people in the street to amuse myself and not be scared. This is Piraeus Street now; it's written on a blue street sign. It's a funny street. I mean they've taken the strangest collection of shops and set them up here: chain saws, driving belts, ball bearings, auto frames. That's all written in big letters above the shops. And there's more: chandeliers, foam rubber, commercial refrigerators, repairs of every kind, we buy and sell all tyres. The people, some in overalls, others in work clothes, go in and out of the shops. Men in suits are standing at the bus stops. On little carts they sell bread-rings and cheese pies. One man, he must be a waiter, shoots across the road carrying a round tray without bothering about the traffic.

Outside a church they've stretched a large sheet that says CONTRIBUTE TOWARD THE COMPLETION OF THE HOUSE OF GOD.

A dirty street. That's to say, it's both grey, with nowhere a whitewashed pavement, *and* it stinks of smoke. It's a kind of yellow and blue smoke that smells like carrion.

Now we're somewhere else. It's a round square. Then comes a very wide street. Here they seem to sell nothing but bathtubs and toilet bowls in many different colours. That's luxury for you!

It's almost two o'clock. Are we anywhere near to where we're going, I wonder? Father asks the driver whether we have still a long way to go. No, he says, he'll turn into Limnos Street in a minute and we'll be there.

We're on the big road that's called Patission Street. There are no words to describe what's going on here. Big yellow buses, blue buses, cars of all colours, you can go crazy. On a corner a shop sells flowers, *real* flowers!

On Symi we have no such shops. Whatever flowers we need, we pick in our gardens: violets for the Epitaphios, lilies for the Annunciation, chrysanthemums for St Demetrius Day, roses and other special flowers for our own patron Saint Panormitis. Only for weddings do they bring flowers from Rhodes. In our garden I have my own flowers. Grandma Eleni had given me a passion plant that we call "the clock". It's a vine and its flowers look like real little clocks. At the bottom of the garden, by the wall, my mother grows parsley, mint, celery, dill, and rose geraniums. The rose geraniums we grow to scent quince jam with.

The car stops. In front of us there is another car that has stopped and beyond that a big yellow vehicle.

"Damn those school buses," says our driver irritated. What on earth are school buses? I see a child in a

40

school smock getting off the vehicle with a lady who takes him to the door of a house and delivers him to an old granny. I say, could it be that in Athens kids go to school by bus? Heavens no, not my cup o' tea! I must tell Father. For me it's *walking* to school!

In between curses our driver says he can't "'mbark" here. What does he mean "'mbark"? We say this when getting on a ship. "It's them trucks 'mbarked all over the place," he says. We had better hurry getting out of the taxi; here's number 101 that we're looking for. Father pays 204 drachmas and the driver unloads our suitcases. The taxi goes off.

We're standing in a very long street. There are more cars here than people. And how tall the houses are! Don't those who live high up there get dizzy?

A lady pushes me aside. "Move along," she says, "you're blocking the pavement."

Father puts the suitcases down on some marble steps. Next to the steps are doorbells, a lot of doorbells. We must ring where it says "Saridis". That's the name of Maria's husband. Father finds the name and rings the bell. There's a buzz and the big door opens. We go in, put down our suitcases and wait. Presently Maria comes down. I know her; she comes to Symi every summer.

"Welcome," she says, "let me show you the way to Stavro's flat where you can leave your things. Then you come up to us for a meal."

She points to a small staircase on the right. We go down the stair. (Where are you, Sotiria, to see how grand it all is!) Only it's dark. Maria switches the light on. It's a long passage-way with doors left and right.

We get to the end of the passage, and Maria opens a door. I can't see anything, it's pitch black. She switches on a light.

"Here's the entrance hall," she says. There's a metal frame bed with a chair beside it.

"Here," she says stepping into another larger room, "is the bedroom." In it there are two camp beds, a small table, three chairs, and a wooden wardrobe. Here too we switch on the light, because it's dark.

"The kitchen, the bath," says Maria pointing. I say, that's real luxury. When we want hot water, she says, we turn this knob. When we've relieved ourselves we pull this chain and water will flush the toilet. (Wish you were here, Sotiria, to see all this!) "And this door leads to the light shaft," says Maria, showing us a door in the kitchen. She suggests we freshen up a bit and then come upstairs to her flat on the second floor to have a meal.

Maria leaves us. We're alone now. Mother asks Father to open the shutters and let in some light. We open the bedroom window, but nothing happens. Only a dim light comes into the room. We still need the electric light to be able to see anything at all. The hall has no window; neither does the bathroom.

We go into the kitchen and open the door. We step out into a tiny courtyard, the size, say, of a chicken coop. It's surrounded by walls and pipes. Next to one of the pipes grows a slender fig tree up to my height. Bless me, Saint Panormitis, what a well shaft this is rising above me! It's really like being in the bottom of a well and looking up at the well head. Mother and Father go indoors again. After the journey we all need to pee, wash our hands and faces and then go up to Maria's who's expecting us. "We'll tidy up afterwards," says Mother.

42

I know my mother. When she puts on this manner, it means, "I don't like it, but I'll do my best to come to terms with it." It was the same that time when we lost our Little Manoli. She shuts her lips tight and plunges into work.

We take a jar of thyme honey from our own beehives, some mountain tea and butter biscuits out of the bag. These are for Maria. We leave the flat. Father locks the door and takes the key. On Symi the house key was always hanging on the wall, and the door was never locked. Why does Father have to lock up here? Well, I'll ask him later, first about the yellow school bus, then about the key.

Now we're going up a wide staircase to the second floor, "storey", as Maria called it. We find the bell that says "Saridis" and ring. Kyriako, her husband, answers the door. Hugs, kisses. Kyriako goes fishing with his cousin Vassili when he comes to the island in the summer. He used to go fishing, that is, because he's had heart trouble for the past three years, and Maria doesn't let him go fishing any more. She argues that if he caught a big fish, the excitement might make him drop dead on the spot.

Her flat is almost like ours, only somewhat bigger. It's got one more room and a little more light. I noticed they've got a TV too.

"This way," says Maria ushering us into the dining room.

Good for you, Maria, I had no idea you were so well off: a wooden sideboard, no less, a dining table with six chairs; a couch as well, a coffee table and a chandelier

43

too! The table is laid for a meal with a pale blue tablecloth. She's made chicken soup for us, because it's good for you after you've been travelling. She knows what's best, being a nurse. She used to be, that is, for now that she's old she looks after her daughter's kids. And we should eat directly, she says, before the baby wakes up and the older boy comes back from school. It's a quiet moment now for us to have our meal in peace.

While eating I have a good look around. What a lot of fancy ornaments! On the floor in the corner there's a vase with ears of corn dyed red, blue, and green. On the couch sits an enormous doll with golden curls and dressed in a long pink dress. She's wearing a picture hat too. On the sideboard there's a row of postcards leaning against the wall. Next to them two gold picture frames with wedding photos, and a clown and some tiny elephants made of glass. There's also a green vase with a bunch of plastic flowers like those in the photographer's studio at Yalos back in Symi.

When you go there to be photographed after a wedding ceremony the photographer places those baskets with plastic flowers to the left and right of you. The poor man can't afford to have real flowers all the time. And, after all, where would he find them? Yet you'll be surprised how good the plastic flowers look in the pictures. I was maid of honour at Helen and George Vassilas' wedding. My mother had made a beautiful tulle dress for me. I wore a small flower wreath on my head (they too had to be artificial flowers) and carried a little basket full of rose petals and rice to shower on the bride and groom. Sotiria's dress had come from Rhodes. It was a taffeta

44

dress and nicer than mine. I'd cried secretly when I saw it laid out on the bed. It had a flounce round the hem too and cloth flowers sewn on all over it. But in the wedding picture Sotiria is sitting beside the bride, and the bride's train covers her taffeta dress, while me, I'm standing beside the groom and, in actual fact, looking at him. That's what the photographer said I should do. The bride was looking at him too. Sotiria was looking at the bunch of flowers the bride was holding. The bridegroom was looking straight into the camera. You can see my hair too, which on that day was not braided but in loose corkscrew curls set with lemon and sugar water. If you add sugar and squeeze some lemon into the water you use for setting your locks, when they dry they hold their shape stiff as candles. The curls are so stiff, you can hardly move your head. Later I'll have a closer look at these Athens wedding pictures to see what the maids of honour look like.

"Go on. Start eating, Astradeni," says Maria. "What are you holding your spoon up in the air for; don't you like my chicken soup maybe?"

I put my head down and start eating. It's the first time I eat in somebody else's house. The others don't stop talking during the meal. My mother asks where the grocery is, so we can do some shopping. Right across the street, says Maria, is a big "supermarkey" (that's what she called it), a big grocery store, that is. They've got everything. You pick things up yourself and then pay the cashier. It opens at six in the evening. I won't miss this for anything. I'll go along with Father when he goes shopping. There's a butcher's there too, and deep-frozen

45

fish, and fruit. That shop's really got everything. Well, that's Athens all right; just as I thought.

"And on Monday," Father says, "we'll enrol Astradeni in school, so she won't miss any classes."

"There's a good school just up the road, on the corner," says Maria.

We were eating apples for dessert when the baby woke up. Maria brought it into the dining room. It's called Philip, and he's a quiet child. His mother works as an accountant in a big textile firm. She leaves at a quarter to seven in the morning and comes back at four in the afternoon. Every other Saturday she has a day off. Maria says she's overworked, but what can she do? If Eleni, her daughter, stopped working, they wouldn't be able to manage. Philip laughs and stuffs his mouth with bread soaked in the salad dressing. And as long as they have only the little one in the house, Maria says, it's all right. But any minute now young Kyriako, the rebel, will arrive.

"Too lively," Maria says. "He's jealous of the baby and pinches it all the time."

At that moment the doorbell rings twice. In comes a little squirt with glasses. Just a little kid and wearing glasses! Wait and see. If he tries any of that smart-alec stuff on me, we're certainly not going to get on at all, the two of us.

And lo and behold, he behaves as if we don't even exist! He ignores our presence completely. Not even so much as a how-d'you-do.

"What's there to eat?" he asks his grandma.

"Chicken soup that you like," she says.

46

He mumbles something that sounds like "The hell I like it."

"Aren't you going to say hello?" his grandpa says. "This here is Astradeni. These are Nicola and Katerina. They've just come from Symi."

"Sure, that's obvious," says the squirt. "I'm in first year primary at school," he says turning to me. "I can read both capitals and small letters."

I feel like saying, "Well, well, that's quite a feat," but I just say, "Good for you, I'm in the fifth year."

Father gets up and says it's time for us to go, so as not to impose on them. We agree to come back for a leisurely cup of coffee in the afternoon, after the children are gone.

We went back to Stavro's flat. Behind the kitchen door there was a broom, and a pail and mop. The place was filthy.

"They can't help it, men living alone," said Mother and rolled up her sleeves.

Out to the little courtyard went table, chairs, camp beds, mattresses. We swept the floor. I counted eight cockroaches. We'll buy some vermin killer when we go to the supermarkey. I detest cockroaches. We mopped the floors and then made the beds. I am to sleep in the metal-frame bed, Father and Mother on the camp beds. I hung my little holy pictures over the head of the bed, Saint Panormitis and Our Lady, as well as the bit of palm leaf I saved from Palm Sunday. On the chair I put my school bag bursting with books. I've also brought my embroidery that I hadn't quite finished before we left home.

Mrs. Antigone said we should all bring along one of the old traditional patterns from home. The boys were to use them for jig-saw work, the girls for embroideries. Most boys brought patterns copied from old carved picture frames. They were full of leaves, birds, and flowers. The girls lifted patterns from old cushions, aprons, and towels. My grandma Eleni, who did a lot of weaving, had lots of beautiful patterns, but they were all needle-point and cross-stitch, and I wanted flatpoint to make the pattern stand out in relief. Finally I settled for my favourite pattern from an old towel, *tsevrés,* as the old-timers call it. In the corner at one end there's a cypress with all its greenery and cones. Next to it is a copper jug full of carnations and two birds perched on them. Then comes a chapel with two arched windows (like the ones at Saint Constantine's chapel) and a Greek cross on top, and again two birds as big as the chapel perched on its roof.

Mrs Antigone said we should guard these and all other old embroideries we have at home like the apple of our eye. And she said we should not exchange our old icons and copper for new things offered to us by salesmen, because they gave us only glossy pictures printed on paper in the place of the icons that our ancestors had worked so hard to create. The same with the copper utensils that decorate our mantelpieces, and our hand-woven kelims, and our traditional island dresses.

"We've come to the point of selling out," said Mrs. Antigone angrily. "Soon we'll be selling our very selves."

I know why she talked like that. When they asked our friend Dimitri to sell his two-storey house down at Yalos, he said, "I'm not selling it, it's my old family home." But afterwards when they offered him double the price, he forgot it was his old family home and let it go.

There's a gentleman who comes to Yalos every spring. At a glance he picks out the houses he fancies and starts, "Will you let me have your house? I'll renovate it without cost to you, I'll let it to the tourists, and I'll give you fifty thousand per year. This arrangement will be binding for ten years only. After that the house will be all yours again.''

Many people make their houses available to the tourists in this way. Others sell them to another gentleman from Athens. He in turn sells them to the Germans, Swedes, Americans. Father says there's some funny business involved, seeing that we're a frontier island opposite Turkey, and the law says no foreigner may own property in a frontier area.

For some such reason too, even the army stationed here are dressed like gendarmes. These gendarmes are considered *the* great lovers on our island. The girls just about melt away when they see them in their uniforms. Strange and scandalous things are known to have happened, but the less said about that the better.

I don't fancy those men in uniform at all. I've seen them many times in their swimming trunks on the beach, and I couldn't care less about them. When you see them like that, all their grand, dignified airs are gone. As Sotiria's elder sister says: plain, ordinary men, that is, not even good-looking.

Well, I fancy a boy I know too. He's in the sixth year at school. Will he be thinking of me, I wonder, now that I'm living in Athens? Last year he was chanting all during Holy Week in the church of Saint Athanasius. Everybody admired his voice. But he was always looking at *me* when he was going humm- hmm, holding the tuning tone. Will he be remembering me now?

I must have fallen asleep. Mother's nudging me. She's sitting on the edge of the bed.

"Wake up, it's time to go shopping with your father." I jump up at once and tidy my skirt. I'm still wearing my best dress. I mustn't forget the cockroach killer.

Mother says, "We need detergent, washing-up liquid, rice, coffee and sugar. And a tin of milk, and toilet paper, and paper napkins. Tomato paste and a bottle of olive oil."

We take along the white calico bag to carry the shopping in.

We go up the narrow stairs in the house and walk out into the street. Such a lot of cars, an awful lot of cars. Some are parked, others are driving past all the time. And the pavements are so crowded. Small kids in school smocks, carrying school bags, are streaming down the pavement like a river. It's as though you've turned on a tap and kids are flowing out. Strange, there are just kids on the pavement, and they're all going downhill. Where are they going at this time of day, six o'clock in the evening? Can it be they're in school from morning till now? Can it be they have more classes in Athens than we had on Symi, that they learn more than we do?

Father takes me by the hand and we cross the street. So this is the supermarkey. Golly, what a shop this is, it's enormous! I stop in front of the window and look inside. Gosh, shelves full of things from floor to ceiling. Father pushes the door open and we go inside. And what a lot of lights! Not even at the Symi Club at Christmas are there are so many lights.

Our way is barred by a kind of metal fence. I stop and look at Father. He stops too. A stocky gentleman in a gabardine coat approaches us.

"You'll leave your bag here, please," he says.

"But we need it for our shopping," Father tells him.

"We'll supply you with shopping bags. Other bags are not allowed in the shopping area. Here's the police order," he says pointing to a sheet of paper posted on the wall.

We leave the bag behind where the gentleman has told us to. We walk in by pushing a cross-shaped metal bar that turns. Only one person can cross at a time, so willy-nilly you must go through all by yourself.

When they do the shearing up in the sheep pens, that's how they do it, but without metal bars, of course. The man who does the shearing sits at one end. The shepherd has gathered the unshorn sheep in the small pen and lets them out one by one, and the shearer takes hold of them, buckles them down in the way he knows, and in a jiffy the sheep is shorn. Then the sheep goes into the other pen, where all the shorn ones are gathered. If you don't do it this way the wool will scatter and get dirty. And you'll waste time trying to find which sheep are shorn and which aren't. That's what you must do in a sheep pen. But why must people enter one by one here?

"We'll pick up the things by ourselves, as Maria said, and then we'll pay, won't we, Father?"

"Yes," says Father. "Here, first of all, is coffee; let's find our brand."

How on earth are we going to find our coffee? There are thousands of big and small tins, big and small packets, all with foreign writing on them. Father picks up a small packet of LOUMIDIS coffee and we move on.

We need rice, sugar — dear me, what a lot of biscuits! I can't see what it says on the packets, but I see on them oranges, cherries, chocolate pouring onto biscuits. I can see hazelnuts, young girls in local costume standing in front of windmills, dew drops on chocolate, a lady putting a biscuit tray in the oven — biscuits, biscuits everywhere.

"Father ..."

"All right, take a packet of biscuits... No, not that one... Take this one."

This one we had on Symi too, it's PAPADOPOULOS BISCUITS. I wanted the other one with the girl in front of the windmill. But I say nothing; Father will only take that much.

We go on. Now it's jams, then come crisps of all sorts, the so-called shrimpies and cheese balls, my mouth waters.

"Look, Father, shrimpies."

"I've seen them. O.K., take a packet. Take a chocolate bar with almonds too, the kind you like, to celebrate our arrival in Athens. But I don't want to hear, Father this and Father that, again," he says and his eyes are smiling.

"What are you carrying the things in your arms for? Take a basket to put your shopping in."

It's the stocky gentleman in the gabardine coat. He speaks very sternly. It seems a gabardine coat always goes with strictness. Just like Mr. Evangelos, our former school principal; he was stern and he wore a gabardine coat. He'd come to us from Athens, from "the city of Athens," as he himself put it. And he insisted that we call him "Mr. Evangelos", and not Mr. Vangeli, which he considered too familiar. Fortunately he only stayed a year before he retired and left.

We're standing in front of a big refrigerator and a counter. A lady in a white smock sells meat. I've never seen a woman butcher before. And there's nothing she doesn't sell: chickens, pork, lamb, goat's meat, rabbit — I read all this on signs hanging everywhere.

"One kilo of deep-frozen minced meat, please," says Father. But Mother didn't ask us to get minced meat. Never mind, he must know.

"Here's olive oil, Father. There's also vinegar and salt. Mother didn't mention salt and vinegar; she'll have forgotten. Shall we get some?"

"Yes, of course," says Father.

We put a bottle of vinegar and a bag of salt in our basket. Before us now is a glass case with sausages. I've always thought mortadella is the only kind of sausage there is; well, maybe spam too. But here, behind the glass, I'd say there are at least fifty different varieties of sausages: reddish ones with small white spots, some with olives pressed in them, large hams, big fat sausages, smaller ones in little nets. Golly, they have it good in Athens! I was right about it all along.

Father has walked on toward the glass case with the cheeses. And here's another surprise. It certainly looks as though there are more cheeses than cream cheese, feta, kefalotyri and kasseri. I'd always thought that was all. But just look at the many cheeses here. One of them is quite mouldy, but they're selling it just the same!

"Half a pound of feta," says Father. "Your mother forgot about feta," he says to me and winks.

We put the feta in the basket and now we're looking for rice and sugar. On some shelves there's pasta and next to it rice. What sort shall we take? Father and I look at each other. We take a green packet and some spaghetti. Further down there are thousands of tins of milk, on a counter thousands of bags of sugar. We pick up a bag of sugar as well and keep going. A turn in the passage and we come to a section full of orange and lemon juices, beer, wines. We can't find tomato paste anywhere. We ask a young woman in a pale blue smock.

"You've missed the tomato section," she says as if she's scolding us. "It's next to the pasta."

We backtrack. Sure enough, tomato tins are next to the pasta shelves. There are tins with pictures of peeled tomatoes, whole tomatoes, tomato juice, and all with different kinds of foreign writing on them. Which is the paste? Father and I exchange looks again. There's a lady shopping next to us. She takes down a red tin. We do the same. Since the lady's taking it, it must be good. And now we're finished at last.

Following Maria's instructions, we go to the cashier to pay now. We find the cashier after going past many more shelves but without stopping at all on the way. At the cashier's we stand behind a gentleman. Ahead of him is a young woman. They place their baskets beside the cash register. The girl in the pale blue smock who's sitting at the cash register takes the things out of the basket one by one, presses some buttons and says

"986.50 drachmas". The young woman pays, takes her things and goes. It's the turn of the gentleman in front of us now. He's bought two bottles of wine and toilet paper. We forgot the toilet paper. What do we do now? I'll tell Father.

"I'm going to fetch some," he says. "You stay here and watch our basket."

The gentleman ahead of us has finished now. He's paid, taken his things and gone away. What do I do now? Father's nowhere to be seen. The lady behind me pushes me.

"Go ahead, child. What are you standing there like that for? Are we to await your pleasure?"

There he is again, the stocky gentleman in the gabardine coat.

"What's the matter here? Why the delay? What are you doing there, little girl?"

"My father... he's gone to get some paper..." I'm afraid of the gentleman in the gabardine coat.

"Put your basket on the counter. Stella, add up the bill."

And what if Father isn't back by the time Stella's finished adding up the bill? What will the gentleman do with me then? "642.20", says Stella and pushes our things toward the other girl who puts them in a bag. What happens now?

"This too," shouts Father coming up and holding out the toilet paper.

Gosh, how embarrassing! Now everybody's looking at us and knows what we wipe our bottoms with. Of course, everyone wipes his bottom with something. But these people know now that we wipe our bottoms with *this* paper.

"654.70", says Stella.

Father takes out the envelope with our money and hands her a thousand-drachma note. He puts the change back into the envelope, we pick up our two bags and get out.

It was awfully nice at the supermarkey with all those thousands of goodies there, if only it weren't for the stocky gentleman in the gabardine coat.

When we got back home Mother was hanging up our clothes in the wardrobe. We put the bags on the table and unpacked the shopping.

"There you are," said Father, "all you wanted and some more. We bought some minced meat and spaghetti for Sunday dinner; some feta cheese, vinegar and salt too."

I take my crisps, biscuits, and my chocolate bar and go to my bed. Mother's already made it up with the blankets we found in the house. But for a bed cover she's used a blanket my grandma Eleni had woven. It's white with blue stripes and tassels. I place my treasures on it and look at them. I'm not going to open them now. No, I'm going to feast my eyes on them first. On Sunday I'll open the chocolate, and I'll take the crisps to school as Sotiria used to do.

Most kids brought food from home with them to school. Some, bread and cheese, others, bread with margarine or jam. But Sotiria and two or three others always brought crisps or potato chips. They did this every day. They were eating them one by one looking at us as if to say, "I'm eating crisps, you're eating bread," which was supposed to mean, "I'm ever so superior."

That's why I'm going to take the crisps to school. But I could eat a piece of chocolate today and the rest on Sunday. No, no, better on Sunday. What pretty wrapping paper the chocolate has; pomegranate-red and brown. I've always wanted a pair of pomegranate-red shoes with low heels and a button-down strap across the instep. They'd brought such a pair from Rhodes to Eleni Tsavari and I liked it ever so much. You couldn't get such shoes on Symi. Maybe... no, not maybe, they'll have them here for sure. If Father has got a job by then, he'll buy me a pair for Easter. Yes. I'll ask him.

In the middle of the chocolate wrapping there are flowers and it says ION in capital letters. Above that it says in gold letters, "Milk chocolate with almonds". So the flowers underneath are almond blossoms. But they haven't painted them properly. The flowers should've been a deeper pink. Inside a circle it says "20 Drs." and inside a square "Vacuum packed. Net weight 64 gr".

On the back there's foreign writing that I can't read. Well, no kidding, I must learn English now that I've come to Athens. In the supermarkey everything's written in English. How else will I know what I'm buying?

Dear consumer,
Our chocolates leave our factory in excellent condition.
Stored properly in a dry, cool place, far from strong
smells and insects, they will remain in prime condition
at least till the expiry date given. If our product is found
lacking in any way, please return it to us for replace-
ment, informing us of the place of purchase. EXPIRY
DATE 30.9.78.

It's the end of March now. The ninth month is... let me figure. June, when school closes, is the sixth month, July's the seventh, August the eighth, so September's the ninth. It's all right then, the chocolate's fresh. Yes, but if it's gone off just the same? I remove the outside wrapper, then the silver foil. Hmm, it looks all right. Well, I'll have a little piece and the rest on Sunday. I won't swallow it at once; I'll let it melt slowly in my mouth. Hmm, fantastic! But not enough of it. I'll have another little piece, because it's sticking out, and I won't be able to wrap it up properly.

Oh blast; the bar has broken in half. Well, then I'll eat the half I've already started on. Half a chocolate bar for Sunday will do quite nicely. As soon as I've wrapped up the chocolate again, Father calls to say it's time to go to Maria's for coffee.

We go upstairs again. Someone's cooking stuffed cabbage leaves; the whole passage smells of them. We haven't had stuffed cabbage leaves for a long time. On Symi we also make *yaprakia,* stuffed cyclamen leaves, that is. All Symians living in Athens ask for *yaprakia* when they visit the island. They can only have them if it's the right season, of course. I wonder about these stuffed cabbage leaves that I can smell here; do they serve them with egg-and-lemon sauce, or just lemon?

A lady and a gentleman are standing in front of a door. The lady's wearing high heels, long pendant earrings and glasses. She smells of eau de cologne. The smell is so powerful I can't smell the cabbage any more. The lady's also carrying a box wrapped in shiny paper. They must be very rich.

The door opens and out comes young Kyriako of all people. The lady and the gentleman go in. The door closes, a small light comes on, and another light sweeps across the glass in the door. What a peculiar door!

Young Kyriako is with a plump grey-haired lady.

"Hello there, you country bumpkins," Kyriako says as soon as he sees us.

"I'll box your ears, and that'll teach you a thing or two, you donkey!" says the lady. "Just wait till we get home, and I'll deal with you properly."

She comes up to us. It's Eleni, Maria's daughter. She says hello and apologises for her son. He's become insufferable, she says. That's exactly what she called him, "insufferable".

She pulls him by the sleeve, and they go away. She keeps muttering to him all the time, "I'll send you to a reformatory to make a decent human being of you, to a reformatory..." What might this reformatory be? I'll ask Father.

"This is the lift," says Father pointing to the peculiar door. I'll take you down in it from Maria's so you can see how it works. Your mother won't go in it; she's afraid."

"And how does it go down?" I ask him.

"You'll see, you'll see," he says, and we walk upstairs. We ring the bell, and Kyriako Senior comes to the door. He's wearing his bathrobe again. It's blue and black check with a satin belt hanging loose. The TV is on.

"Take a seat," says Kyriako. "Maria will be back any moment. She's gone to give an injection."

Father asks how Maria's work is going.

"Now that she could've earned a few pennies, she's too old for it. She can no longer climb all those stairs. She's exhausted looking after Eleni's children as well."

On the TV they're showing "The Greek and His Automobile". A gentleman with necktie and glasses, and a pretty blonde girl are telling us what we must do for our car to consume less petrol. The girl tells us that the Greek Automobile Club can now be of assistance to drivers in Boeotia AS WELL! This must be a very great

61

thing, because the girl's eyes brighten up as if she's proud of it. We have no cars on Symi. How can we, when there are no roads. Now the MOMA, the army construction units that is, are surfacing a road that goes from Yalos to Parnomitis. It'll go past Saint Constantine's as well. A bit in the middle is still unfinished, but when that's done too, well, we'll be hard to beat, because then we'll have a bus too!

Maria comes home with some biscuits. She says they're from the bakery. They taste very good just the same. They're cinnamon biscuits, and I down two of them at once.

Maria's brewing coffee and keeps asking questions: how's Thareini, has Eleni had her baby yet, has Irene's Michali married yet, what did Aleko die of?

I know all that; I prefer to watch TV. The girl leaves. The gentleman says goodbye with a sweet smile and goes too. Now there are lights, many lights. Some in rows going on and off, others rush across the screen in the foreground. Some foreign writing rushes across too and disappears. Some ladies dressed in men's clothes appear. They're wearing dress coats, boutonnieres, top hats, and are carrying canes. They perform all sorts of tricks while dancing, and... oh well, my dear, that's too much... they show their bare bottom! All of it! They turn around suddenly and, hopla, there are all their bottoms in full view. They ought to be ashamed of themselves, grown-up women too. But I daresay it must be the way it's done in dance numbers. Since it's shown on TV, it must be O.K. That second dancer from the right is the prettiest one. She's blond. I pretend it's me. I lift my leg up high. I touch the cane that I'm holding in both hands, and with a bound, hop! I land on the floor with my legs split apart. It must be hard to do. I'll try it downstairs in the flat. The ladies have gone. Now some men come on holding enormous bananas in their hands.

Oh, go on, where did they get them? The bananas are taller than they are. They must be artificial for sure. They hold them above their heads waving them. Now they sit down in a double row forming an arcade with the bananas. Some girls in tulle and feathers appear in the background. They pass under the bananas, and now they're dancing. I'm the one with the feathers on her head; she's the prettiest one. No, no, I'm that one there, the one with the sequins on her bosom. How beautiful these girls are!

"Turn it off, Maria, there's nothing worth watching," says Kyriako Senior.

He calls that not worth watching? I can't imagine what they're showing when it's really good! I must manage somehow to visit Maria more often.

Maria switches off the TV. She sits opposite me on the couch. We're sitting in another room, without a window, not the dining room where we had lunch. It's got a couch and two chairs in it. On the walls are some photographs of some children.

"What d'you think of Athens, then, Astradeni?" Maria asks me.

What I think of it... how do I know? It's O.K. It's got cars and noise that I don't like. As for Stavro's flat... I don't know...

"It's fine," I say. What else should I say? If Maria's living here, it means she likes it.

"But Symi's better," says Maria. "It's quiet, it's got the sea, fresh air, beautiful houses and nice people."

She's confusing me now. If she likes Symi so much,

what's she living in Athens for? Of course, when Maria comes in the summer, that's the way she sees things, everything's beautiful! And it's true enough: sea, fresh air, quiet. But in winter, Maria ma'am, in winter the sea grows wild, and the island's cut off from the rest of the world. You can't even go to Rhodes. No doctor, no decent jobs. But what's the point of telling her.

"Are you thinking of going to sea?" Kyriako asks Father. Mother's eyes flash looking from Kyriako to Father. She's hanging on Father's lips waiting to hear his answer.

"Out of the question. I couldn't leave the girls behind alone," he says looking at us with a smile. "I'm going to my *koumbaro* Noufri Sunday afternoon. He lives in Perama. There may be something at the shipyards, he says."

"Give him my phone number," says Maria. "He can contact you here about a job, and I'll call you to the phone."

"It's hard to get anything at the shipyards," Kyriako says. "There are no jobs. If you were willing to sail..."

No, he's not willing to sail; we've settled that one. A good job, yes, but not on a ship. What, me becoming like Eleni's Lefteritsa, whose father keeps sending her presents but doesn't ever come himself? Lefteritsa's even got a SEIKO watch, *and* a camera, *and* American bedsheets with rubber bands to fit around the mattress, *and* Chinese tablecloths. The only thing she hasn't got is her father. She doesn't even remember what he looks like. He hasn't been back to see them for four years. He left a ten-year-old child behind, and she's a girl of fourteen now. To say nothing of how something may happen to him on the ships, see, like to poor Lefteraki, God rest

64

his soul. Well, God forbid, but let me knock on wood too without anyone noticing. Yes, and what happened to Uncle Sotiri's Yanni was no less awful.

The boy was doing his watch twelve to four in the morning, when, suddenly, three black Senegalese rushed on to the bridge. They were wearing some sort of towel around their waist and their eyes were shining. Yanni says they were stoned, drunk, that is.

"The captain is too cruel," said the Senegalese, "so we're knocking him off."

And they pulled knives that big! Yanni wet his pants with fear. There was a sailor from Piraeus on the bridge with Yanni... They looked at each other and attacked. They managed, finally, to disarm the Senegalese, but not before they had cut one ear off of the Piraeus sailor and slashed the whole length of Yanni's arm. I've seen the scar with my own eyes, a white line that goes from his shoulder down to his wristwatch.

No sir! We can do without the ships. Now they hire foreign crews anyway, coloured men and Africans. It's so bad, you can do your two watches without speaking to a soul, in Greek, that is. Well, I ask you, what sort of life is that on board under such conditions? No, not the sea. Let him find something else, even if it means less money. I'm sure our *koumbaro* will arrange things alright on Sunday. He's got his ways and means. Let me eat another biscuit.

"And you, Katerina, are you thinking of working?" Maria asks Mother.

My mother smiles shyly and smoothes her skirt over

her knees. She remains silent. My father answers for her.

"Katerina's staying at home. We'll treat her like a queen. Here in Athens especially, where she'll have every convenience, it's worth her staying at home. No wood to gather for the laundry fire, no oven to heat, no bread to knead, and no weaving. Everything on the spot at the supermarkey, Madame Katerina, just across the street from your flat," says Father and seems in high spirits.

"We'll see, we'll see," says my mother.

I can't sit on this couch any longer. My feet are hanging in the air and are hurting. I wish they had a yard I could go out to, and a kid my age.

In the afternoons, on Symi, Alemina sometimes came to our house, or we went to Eleni's, or all of us together went to Zopighi's. Our mothers were busy with afternoon chores. Some were knitting, some were shredding rags to weave them into rugs, others were making lace, except when, at certain times of the year, they had a chore to do in common and they all worked together at it, like shelling almonds, or lentils, or beans, or making biscuits or noodles.

Us kids played in the yard when the weather was good. Otherwise we sat beside them on the *apokrevatto* in the kitchen where it was warm. I liked both. In the yard we played hop-scotch, or statues, or house. In the kitchen we played house or school. That was fun too, because, while you were playing, you could listen in on the mothers' conversation. Back home on Symi kitchens aren't as skimpy as they're here. The kitchen's a big room, a very big room, where we do all our work. We even sleep there in winter when it's cold. At one end is the *apokrevatto,* a raised built-in bed. It's a kind of platform one metre high. Three steps lead up to it, and it's got a railing along the edge. It keeps the children sleeping there from falling off. We spread colourful rugs on it and played house barefoot, so as not to dirty the rugs. Under the *apokrevatto* there's storage space where we keep a lot of things. We also threaten the little ones that we'll shut them up in there if they don't behave, and their fear of the bogeyman or the old witch makes them behave.

My parents sleep high up in a bed that you reach by climbing fifteen steps. At the other end of the room is the hearth and beside it the water tap from the cistern. We don't light the hearth very often, seeing that it's never really very cold on Symi. The cold is not worth worrying about. You drink some mountain tea and you feel warm in a jiffy. We only light a fire in the hearth at Christmas for good luck, for smoke to rise in the chimney and drive out evil spirits and chase the goblins away. The rest of the time we've got the propane gas cooker in the hearth for cooking. Next to the hearth is the window. On Symi windows are different. I noticed this as soon as we arrived in Athens and was surprised. Here the windows are — how should I say — sort of thin. Back home they have a very wide window sill on the inside. We keep lots of things there. In fact, in the kitchen, the sink is built into one of the window sills. Its bottom is slanted outward, and there's a wide slit through which the soapy water runs out.

Under the window we plant aubergines, mint, basil, marigolds. Soapy water is great for flowers and vegetables. It's fertilizer, as Father says. It makes them grow lush and tall. So dishwater is not wasted as here. For God's sake, where does all this water go to here? Don't they feel sorry for wasting it? But how silly of me, what should they be feeling sorry for? Here they turn the tap on and the water runs like anything. They needn't worry about a cistern that they may drain dry and be left without water. In any case cistern water is the best. It's God's rain, as the old-timers say. It's beautiful, sweet water. It makes wonderful lather, and it's great for washing your hair. This Athens water, it smells funny; it tastes different too, like medicine.

Of course, you've got to watch out with your cistern water. You must manage to make it last through the summer and have some left over for washing blankets and rugs.

"Come, Astradeni, time to go," says Father. He's got up already and so has Mother. I stand up shaking the biscuit crumbs from my lap.

"And as I said," Maria tells Father, "give Noufri my phone number."

"Thanks, Maria," Father says. We say goodbye and leave.

"Let's go down in the loft," I say to Father.

"*Lift*," he corrects me. "O.K. then let's go. Katerina, you go down the stairs and wait for us below."

We go to the lift door and he presses a button. A red light and a green arrow light up. Then the glass in the door is lit up. Father opens the door and we get in. The door closes by itself. I'm scared. Why did the door shut by itself? What if it doesn't open again? Father presses a button beside the letters GF, and I'm suddenly shook up. If Father hadn't held me, I'd 've fallen down.

"Where are we going?" I ask. I must look scared, because Father's stroking my head.

"We're there already. The lift has taken us down two floors without the least effort on our part."

The least effort indeed! As if twenty steps, and going down too, is an effort. It was too stuffy in there; I didn't like it. And if something goes wrong with the buttons, or the door won't open? I can do without the lift; I'll walk up and down the stairs like Mother.

"Where's Mother?" I ask. "She should've been here by now."

"Katerina!" Father shouts.

"Here I am," her voice comes from the distance.

"Where are you, have you gone downstairs?"

"Yes!"

"Let's go," says Father.

We go down the broad stairs in the hall. There are lots of lights here. There are three flowerpots too with small pieces of mirror stuck in their sides. Some strange flowers grow in them. I must take a closer look at them tomorrow. We go down our own little staircase. Now it's pitch black and we can see nothing. We walk down the passage fumbling.

"The light switch must be here somewhere," Father says.

"Mother!" I call out.

Nothing, no answer. I don't like it down here. It's dark and stuffy. You feel the passage walls closing in on you.

"Whatever's happened to your mother? She should be here," Father says with anxiety in his voice.

"Astradeni, you stay here. I'm going upstairs again.

I'll find the switch and turn the light on. Your mother must be on the first floor. I'll be back in a minute.''

And here I am, alone in this dark tunnel. I'd be lying if I say I'm not scared. Suppose the bogeyman or the old witch appears. Shame on you, Astradeni, I say to myself, that's baby stuff. Yet I feel as though there's a flapping of wings here beside me. My heart's beating fit to burst. I don't suppose it's a bat. How could there be bats in Athens. There aren't any bats in Athens. I'm scared to death of bats.

It was Eleni, Sotiria's sister, who once suggested we should go to the country chapel of Saint Noulias, where there are lots of bats, and catch a couple of them. We would then pin them down on a piece of board and leave them outdoors till they died and were eaten by the ants. When just the bones were left, we would pick out the little bat bone that works as a charm. We would wear it as a talisman, because it brings you luck in everything, and most of all in love. In those days Eleni had her eye on a gendarme who didn't seem to take any notice of her.

There's that flapping of wings again. I can't actually hear it, but I feel it as if it's going right past me fanning my face. And that light, why hasn't Father found it yet?

We'd been told you must catch the bats at dusk, because that's when the virtue of their little bone is most concentrated.

So we started out at about six in the evening. We said we were going to gather wood for Sotiria's mother. She needed wood all right, but Eleni's need for the bats was greater. We hurried down the steps of the upper town and took the road to Periviotis. Then we took a path on the left. I'd never been to that chapel before. There were no regular services held in it. We were walking between two loose-stone walls that continued all the way to the entrance of Saint Noulias. The yard was surrounded by a low wall built with grey stones that had tumbled down here and there. There was a thick layer of cypress cones on the ground. They were very dry, and I gathered a bag-full. Cypress cones make very good kindling.

The chapel wasn't whitewashed like all our other chapels. It was a red brick building and had two deep dishes of blue china stuck in the wall above the windows. There was no bell. An oblong piece of wood was hanging on a heavy chain beside the door, and next to it a mallet, something like a mallet, that is. As if I'd done it many times before, I took hold of the mallet and started striking the wood. It gave me the shivers. It was getting dark. I kept a beat, tak tak, pause, tak tak tak, and repeated it over and over again. My hand seemed to move of its own accord. "Jesus Christ conquers, and all evil scatters," I said aloud, dropped the mallet, and quickly crossed myself three times.

Eleni and Sotiria pushed the chapel door open and went in. On the right the doorstep was extremely worn down, but I crossed it and entered. There weren't many icons; only the four in the altar screen. There were three oil lamps that hadn't burned for a long time. There was no oil in them. High up in the dome there were two crossed beams. A chandelier must've hung from them once upon a time. Bats were hanging from them now. They came in through the broken panes high up in the dome. The bats grew restless, because we'd disturbed them. Eleni shut the door and, using a stick, tried to

71

make the bats fly. It was very dark in the chapel now. There was a smell of old candles and oil dregs gone rancid in the lamps. There was another smell too, an "old" smell like in a basement. It was chilly, just as it's here right now. And the bats were screeching, flying about agitated. It was frightening. Finally I got so scared, I started screaming.

"Let's get out of here! We'll get some bat tangled up in our hair, and we'll have to have it cut like Vassili's Maria. Let's get out of here!"

There goes that flapping again! For heaven's sake, where's Father?

"Father, Father!"

"Here we are, Astradeni; we're coming."

"Have you found Mother?"

"Yes, of course, and we're coming."

"The light, can't you switch it on?"

A door opens next to me, and a light is switched on. A gentleman in pyjamas, slippers, a jacket thrown over his shoulders, comes out. The woman beside him has orange hair and is wearing a red housecoat with feathers round the cuffs.

"What's wrong, little girl? What are you shouting for?"

At the same time another door opens across the way, and out comes a little old woman with a shawl over her shoulders caught with a safety pin under her chin. Another woman's standing behind her. She's very fat and is dressed in men's pyjamas.

"What's going on here, Mr. Aleko?" asks the old woman.

72

"How should I know," says he looking bored. "This child's screaming." He turns to me, "Who do you belong to?"

I'm dumbfounded. What shall I tell him? What does he mean, "Who do you belong to?"

"Astradeni, are you all right?"

It's Father who appears first on the narrow stairs. Mother comes puffing behind.

"Are you new here?" asks the old woman. "When did you arrive?"

"Just today," says Father.

"And what's the child screaming for in the middle of the night?" asks the gentleman called Aleko fixing me with his eyes.

"We don't know our way around here yet, you see," Father says. "She couldn't find the light switch."

Was it me who couldn't find the switch, Father dear? You said *you* were going to turn the light on. But I say nothing. If Father puts it this way, he must have his reasons.

"Come on, Toula, let's go back in, we'll miss the serial," says the old woman pushing the fat one in the men's pyjamas back into the flat. The gentleman and the lady withdraw too after having muttered, "In the middle of the night! Raising hell in the middle of the night!"

I can't tell you how ashamed I felt. There you are, I lost my nerve and started shouting. I made my parents worry and disturbed the neighbours too. For goodness sake, why should I be scared of the dark and of something flying about? I'm having a good look around now, and there's nothing to see, no bat. I need a good shaking up to come to my senses. And how embarrassing for Father it all was.

"Come, let's go in," Father says and leads us gently into the flat. He locks and bolts the door. We stand in the middle of the room and look at each other.

"My dear girls," says Father putting his arms around both of us. And as if by mutual agreement, Mother and I burst into tears. We stay like this, hugging each other, for some time.

"Mistress Katerina," says Father, "what do you say about brewing us some sage tea to calm our nerves before going to bed?"

We break up our embrace. Mother goes into the kitchen, and I set the table. We drink our hot sage tea with whole-wheat rusks. Then we rinse the cups and tidy up the kitchen.

On my bed Mother has laid out my nightie, my good nightie. Fotara's Irene, who's had sewing lessons, made it for me. It's yellow flannel with white dots. It's nice and warm, except, when I turn in my sleep, it gathers round my waist and bothers me.

I get ready for bed and say my prayers. First I recite, "Lord have mercy upon us", then "Our Father", and finally "Lord, watch over my father, my mother and all our relatives". I put the crisps, the biscuits, and the remaining half of the chocolate bar in my school bag. I tuck myself in and wait. Mother's going to come in now and make the sign of the cross over me and give me a good-night kiss.

There she is. She's standing over me looking very earnest. She makes the sign of the cross over me moving her lips, whispering something. She kisses me on the forehead and says, "Good night, Astradeni."

She leaves the room, switching the light off. My parents settle for the night as well and put their light out.

"Good night, Astradeni."

"Good night, Father."

Total darkness. I open my eyes, I shut my eyes, it's dark all the same. But I'm not scared of this dark. I grow used to it little by little. The oil lamp Mother has lit in the other room in front of Saint Panormitis' icon gives a faint glow. First night in Athens.

I seem to be standing in front of the cypress at the chapel of the Archangel Michael. It's a chapel beyond Periviotis. In front of it there's a big round area, the *flats,* as we call it, surrounded by a low wall. It's where the feasting takes place at weddings, christenings, on Saint Michael's Day. And there in the middle is an odd cypress. It doesn't rise upward like other cypresses, but has spread its branches sideways like an umbrella, because its top has been cut off.

Three women are sitting under the cypress. They're wearing white garments and are barefoot. Their hair hangs loose down to their waists. When they see me, they beckon to me to go near. But I'm scared and stay put. Then they start walking along the path that leads to the chapel. And me, as if an irresistible breeze is pushing me, I start walking toward the chapel. I'm barefoot too, and my dress is very odd. I'm wearing a loose yellow garment like a tunic, like the one Helen of Troy has on in the pictures I've seen. Over it I'm wearing the jacket of our festive local dress, the fur-trimmed one. It's maroon velvet over my yellow tunic. I want my yellow tunic to show, but the jacket is tightly buttoned over it. My head is covered with a light blue kerchief of printed cotton with a purple crocheted fringe around it.

Those women are going on ahead. They don't turn round to see whether I'm following, as if they're sure I'm coming up behind. And it seems as though all of us aren't quite walking on the ground, as though we're half an inch above the ground, floating along.

And there's no sound at all, neither of bird or cricket, nor of human beings, not even any goats bleating. This is the oddest thing of all.

We arrive at Saint Michael's gate, but it isn't the gate that's there now, the wrought-iron one. It's a wooden gate, it seems, made of heavy beams scarred by the rain and with square-headed nails driven into them.

The gate opens by itself. The three women, and me on their heels, enter Saint Michael's courtyard. The gate shuts behind us. I don't hear or see it closing but I'm sure it's shut behind us. We go past the olive press on the right and into the inner yard of the chapel. It's paved with pebbles like black beans. Around the edge and in the corners the pebbles form patterns like crosses and cypresses. It's just as I remember it.

The three women go past the chapel door without stopping. Where are they heading, I wonder. They turn and go down the stairs to the old chapel. Because under the regular chapel at Saint Michael's there's an ancient one. No one knows when it was built. It's got saints painted on its walls and on its vaulted ceiling. Everything's covered with soot, however. It seems there was a fire in the olden days.

Me, I'm too scared to go down there. But the women stand in the door and wait for me. It's at that moment I look into their eyes and am petrified. They're empty! No whites, no pupils, just empty sockets! I'm dreadfully scared, but go down with them just the same.

They've gone on into the chapel. But the chapel's no longer charred by the fire. It's all white, and there are beautiful pillars with capitals on them. We've learned about capitals in school, but now I can't remember to say what kind they are, Doric or Ionic. Anyway the capitals are plain, without ornaments. And the chapel has no wooden altar screen. At the back, in the Holy of Holies, where the altar is, there's a white marble table. It's bare; no altar cloth with embroidered cross. There's only a large censer on it.

Now the three women stand in front of the marble table. They drop something that starts hissing in the censer. They raise their arms above their heads and start speaking words I can't understand. I can only separate out a few words here and there that make sense: Diana, Bear, virgin, sacrifice. Now I'm really scared. The word "sacrifice" scares me most of all. I turn to go. The three women don't bother to try and stop me, as I feared they might. But the door behind me is shut. I start banging and banging on it and crying. I shout, "Mother! Mother!" and keep banging and weeping and screaming. But it seems no sound comes out of my mouth, and this scares me even more, and I toss with anxiety and wake up. It looks as though I've really been crying in my sleep, and I'm drenched with sweat.

I cross myself at once and recite the whole of the "I Believe". I'm too ashamed to wake my mother. What will I tell her anyway? Tomorrow I'll go to the church here to light a candle to the Archangel. Is it possible I made a vow to him and forgot about it? Not likely. Saint Michael wasn't angry. And Diana, how come she was involved; she's an old, an ancient goddess. And the Bear, that's the constellation my father pointed out to me when we were sailing in the caique. It's all very odd. And when it comes to the virgin bit, well, I know all about that. But the sacrifice? The sacrifice worries me.

Let me try and think of something else, because my heart's beating too fast. Golly, what a fright I got! Well, let me think about *koumbaro* Noufri who we're visiting tomorrow. But the sacrifice — who were they going to sacrifice? It was me, wasn't it? It was me for sure. But why, why?

Well now, we're going to Noufri's after lunch. Father said so. It's so they don't think we're starving and are trying to get a free meal.

I wonder what time it is. On Symi, when I woke up in the night, I could roughly guess what time it was. If the oil lamp burned bright, it was not past three in the morning. If it was hissing, then it was almost four or four-thirty. If the oil lamp had gone out, it was nearly five. That was in the winter, of course, because in summer it was daybreak by then anyway, and the cocks were crowing. My mother got up at half past five winter and summer. She gave the chickens food and drink, drew water from the cistern, made sage tea, woke my father. When it was baking day, she got the leaven going first thing. Of course, we have a "German" bakery on the island now. It uses petrol and bakes fresh bread every day. But Father prefers Mother's home-made bread. It tastes better and keeps fresh for five days, while the baker's bread goes dry and stale at once.

I can knead bread too. My mother's taught me. I learned, that is, by watching her. Kneading's an art, but the flour's no good nowadays. They remove all the bran from it, says Mother, and the bread you make doesn't taste as good as it used to. Even if you take your own wheat to the mill, it comes out with the bran removed. They've got tricks to produce two or three kinds of flour out of one sort of wheat. That's what Mother says.

But the preheating of the oven is an art too. You must figure the exact right moment when the loaves go in. You must pile the embers into the special hollow the oven has inside. You must go over the burning hot stones of the oven with a wet cloth. You must arrange the loaves neatly inside and take them out at the right time without opening and shutting the oven door in between. You must give them a shine by going over the crust with water, then place them on the bread board and cover them with a clean sheet.

On baking day, which is mostly Saturday, we also cook some food in an oven dish, while the oven is still hot. We usually cook tomatoes or peppers stuffed with rice if it's summer, spinach pie if it's winter. My mother sets some dough aside and bakes a large spinach pie that's a dream. In the autumn we have to put our figs and prickly pears out in the sun to dry. Then, depending on which is at hand, we put bay or rose geranium leaves between them and push them into the oven. We store them in tins or cloth bags for the winter when there's no fresh fruit. And I must say, when in winter you give them some time on the cast-iron stove or the hot slab of the cooker, you end up with a real delicacy. But what about that sacrifice, and what about Diana?

We're taking some honey over to Noufri's as a present. This year our honey didn't turn out too good. It was because of the oil slick from the ships. It was washed out on to Tolio beach where we kept our beehives, and the whole place turned black. The poor bees got their little feet full of tar, and they produced black wax in the

honeycombs. So our honey's not golden like last year's.
My father had to sell it at a lower price.

"Come. Astradeni, get up, so we can go to church."

My mother's dressed already and has done her hair. Fancy that, I fell into a deep sleep again after the dream. I stretch in bed: it feels good. First Sunday in Athens.

I get up and go to the bathroom to wash. It's cold for March, but here in the bathroom there are some metal rods that are hot. You touch them and they burn your hand. They're like a stove. But where's the fire, I wonder. I pee in the toilet bowl. It's white with a round black lid.

Sotiria had one like that in her house. Nowadays more people at Yalos build toilets in their houses, because the foreign tourists always want a bathroom and toilet when they rent a room. In the end there won't be a house left down at Yalos that isn't let to foreigners. They don't much come our way in the upper town. They have to climb stairs till their tongues hang out. They're not used to climbing, while we're like mountain goats. We can run down to Yalos and back in a jiffy. And we haven't got toilets either, so how should we let rooms?

Well, I must now pull the chain as Maria said. Heavens, what a lot of water, a real waterfall! So much water, just for flushing the toilet? It's out of the question; there must be some additional reason for such wasteful use of water. On Symi, even those who had a regular toilet kept a pail of water in it with a jug, and poured water in the bowl according to need. I say, could

82

it be that this flushing water is meant to wash your bottom too while you're sitting on the bowl? That's what it must be. Well, that's Athens for you; let me try it out.

"Hurry up, Astradeni! Why're you taking so long? Maria's already rung our bell."

O.K., I'll try it another time. I wash in a hurry and come out of the bathroom. I put on the same clothes as yesterday. Mother has shaken and aired them, so they feel quite fresh. My mother's wearing her best black dress and a heavy jacket. She wears nothing but black ever since we lost our Little Manoli. My cousin Sevasti had sent her the jacket from Canada. It was a green and yellow woollen jacket with three big buttons. Mother dyed it black. It shrank in the dying, but my mother's lost weight, so it still fits her. She's holding a folded handkerchief with a black border, which is a sign of mourning, and her small purse with the money for the candles and the collection plate.

"Maria's taking us to church," says Mother. "She'll be down any minute now. Aren't you coming?" she asks Father.

Why bother, since it's the same story every Sunday. "Not today," he always answers. He wouldn't even go with us to Saint Thanassi, our parish church, and she imagines he'll go to this strange church now? Maria rings our bell.

"Are you two ready to go?"

We come out of our flat. Through the neighbours' doors we can hear chanting and priests' voices. Heavens, it looks like they're ill, unable to go to church, so they listen to the service on the radio. We go upstairs. It's bitter cold, the kind of cold we have on Symi in January. It's overcast too. What if it rains? We haven't even got an umbrella. The supermarkey is closed. Except for two or three people, there's not a soul in the streets. All the shops are closed.

"Here, as soon as we turn the corner, we'll see the church of Haghia Zoni."

So that's the name of our new church, Haghia Zoni, the Holy Waistband. What Holy Waistband, I wonder. What saint did the waistband belong to, and why did it become holy? On Symi we have the churches of Saint Thanassi, the Holy Cross, the Holy Trinity, Our Lady of Piraeus, Saint Demetrius, but no Holy Waistband.

"Well, Katerina, will you be able to find your way back?" Maria asks.

"Aren't you coming with us?"

"I've got to give some injections," says Maria. "It's easy to get back. You just turn here see, and you're practically home..."

"All right," says Mother.

She takes me by the hand, and we go on till we come to the courtyard of the church. There's a high wall all around, and the sanctuary of the smaller church is flush with this wall. But the wall looks dirty; and it is dirty. It's not because it isn't whitewashed but painted brown, it's because there's writing in black letters on it. It says, "Coup, 21.4.67, Amnesty". There was more, but it's smeared over. Is there no one here to whitewash the walls properly? What a mess!

The courtyard is paved with big flagstones, but not like the ones we have on Symi. These are square and regularly placed. There are two churches in the yard, a small one on the right and an enormous one in the middle. I've never seen such a big church. It's got coloured glass in the windows and two very tall belfries with four bells. We go into the big church with the rest of the crowd. First we climb some marble steps. Someone's sitting on the right with outstretched hand begging. Another man chases him out saying: "Scram! Get out of here this minute!"

As soon as we're inside the church, a lady presses a sheet of paper into our hands. THE VOICE OF THE LORD, it says. I'll read it after church. Mother picks up four candles and drops a twenty-drachma piece into the box. We move along and light our candles. What a candle stand! It's fantastic. It can take thousands of candles and it's revolving too! My mother lifts me, so I can kiss the icon. The glass is full of lipstick marks. I find a little clean corner and barely touch it with my lips, may God forgive me. We stand on the left, next to the candle stand, where the women are standing. They aren't standing, actually. Some are sitting in the pews and others on folding stools. Tsak! they unfold their stools and sit on them.

What a marvellous church! It's full of coloured glass, chandeliers with electric lights (one with red bulbs too) and gilded icons, and the cantors in lots of five. Only I don't get the words the way they chant. They put too much nose into it, as Father Lemonis used to say, and that doesn't make for a good cantor.

And the people! What a difference to Symi. The ladies, even the old ones, are wearing beautiful fur-trimmed coats, hats, gloves, brooches, rings, high heels. I'm watching them as they come to light their candles here at the candle stand next to us. Mother's nudging me all the time, because I'm not paying attention to the ser-

85

vice. But I can't make out the words anyway. They chant in unison, and it's all through the nose.

The sacristan, a woman, comes, grabs a whole lot of candles from the stand and puts them out by dipping them in a saucepan with water. Then she throws them into a pail full of hundreds of extinguished candles. I nudge Mother saying, "She's put out our candles!" My mother shakes her head and presses her lips together. The sacristan repeated this performance eight times before the end of the service. She did another thing too. With a piece of cotton wool, that must've been wet, she wiped the lipstick marks off the icon.

A little girl came in dressed to the nines. Just like a LAMBROPOULOS window piece, as our friend Toula used to say. She'd been to Athens and had seen the big department store called LAMBROPOULOS. Since then, whenever she dressed and groomed her son Michali, she said, "You're a doll, child, just like a LAMBROPOULOS window piece." Well, this little girl is a real LAM-BROPOULOS window piece. She's wearing a white over-coat with fur all round the bottom, a hat (fancy that, just a kid and wearing a hat!) with daisies on it. All this with white knee-length socks and patent leather shoes with low heels and button-down straps across the instep. She's carrying a small white purse over her arm. Her hands are tucked into a small round fur piece. If I were wearing all this finery, I'd be a doll, because I'm both taller and better-looking than her. My braid (I've plaited my hair into a single braid today) reaches down to my waist. She's got short hair. But her mother's every bit of a lady. She's put money in all five collection plates that have come around. And what's one to make of that, *five* collection plates? They were brought round by those men who kept saying, "For the completion of the church", "For the Charity Fund", "For the Christian Brotherhood", "For the Home for the Incurables", and I don't know what else. My mother had kept a two-drachma piece in her palm to drop in the collection plate as we do on Symi. She dropped it into the first collection plate. After that the gentlemen with the plates stopped and hesitated in front of her, but my mother kept her eyes lowered. Two hatted old ladies next to her were watching her too as if to say, "Why don't you contribute to the other collection plates as well?" I say, women do really go in for hats in Athens.

But what made the greatest impression on me was Andreas. That's what the sacristan called him. He was elderly and very tall with very hairy fat legs. I could see his legs, because he was wearing shorts. Fancy that, a grown-up man in shorts! His head was shaven and he was barefoot. Yes sir, barefoot in March! I saw him after church. He was sitting out there on a low wall eating a yoghurt, and when the ladies went past he made a sign with his finger and used dirty words. He must've been mad. I was terribly scared of him.

Well, there you are, I couldn't follow the chanting, nor did I listen to the sermon. I was distracted looking around in the big church. I counted the men and women saints painted all over. I counted forty-three women saints and twenty-six men saints, not including those hidden behind pillars and arches. And Christ Pantocrator was very handsome, only He looked a little cross. I wondered why He seemed so cross.

You see, on Symi I knew everybody and all the saints too. There were only a few of them, so I paid attention to the service.

To find our way back home I had taken note of a haberdashery. I knew that was where we had to turn off the main road. I told Mother, and we went around the corner. A lot of people were walking along with us now. An old woman ahead of us was carrying a little stool, and beside us went a gentleman in hat and gloves. There were no cars; only a couple drove past, so the people were walking in the middle of the street. Many of them were carrying newspapers. When we got home, Mother lifted me up, so I could reach the bell with Stavro's name on it. Father came running and opened the door for us. We went downstairs to our flat.

Mother changed into the dress she always wears at home. It's got buttons all down the front, a belt, and pockets on either side. It's black, of course. She took off shoes and stockings. In the house she wears a pair of black plastic slippers. It's always the same clothes as if it's her uniform. She put on her apron and disappeared into the kitchen. I followed her.

"Get out of here," my mother said, "you'll stain your new dress, and then how're we going to go to Noufri's."

"You mean, get out of the kitchen or out of the house?" I said.

"Out!" she said absentmindedly, taking the mince out of Stavro's fridge.

And now, Mistress Astradeni, what are we going to do with ourselves? There's no yard to go out to, no kids to play with, no homework to do — not yet, anyway.

On Symi all of us kids of the neighbourhood got

together to play after church. When it was raining we went to somebody's home to play house. What shall I do now? Suppose I read that pamphlet they gave us in church to help pass the time.

APOSTOLIC DEACONRY OF GREECE, it says at the top in blue letters. Underneath it says, THE VOICE OF THE LORD.

Well, I've read all the articles. I read ALWAYS FORWARD AND UPWARD, PROGRESS OF REGRESSION, THE LITTLE SHEPHERD OF DIMITSANA, INCONSISTENCY OF CHRISTIANS, DO WE LOVE OURSELVES?, EUSTACE, THE GREAT MARTYR.

I've read the whole lot, and now I admire the Athenians even more. Boy, how educated they must be! I mean, we Symians must be really stupid, because I read everything but didn't understand a thing; well, not quite, of course, but nothing much anyway. The pamphlet's full of foreign names too, Hegel, Marx, Freud. The Athenians, well, since they hand it out to them, it means they like it and understand it too. I only understood the bit about the mountain climbers who always keep their eyes fixed on the mountain top. And that other bit that says we're kneeling in the mud and putting our faith in magicians.

There's no doubt about it, I've got to keep my eyes wide open and get educated. Athens without education doesn't work.

"May I go to Maria's?" I ask my mother.

"Go ahead, but behave yourself."

I go out into the passage. Oh boy, what smells of all sorts of meat dishes being cooked! Here, where that old woman and the fat woman in men's pyjamas live, they're roasting chicken. We killed all our chickens on Symi.

Ever since that happened with our Little Manoli, my mother got to hate our chickens. She had seen the signs. A month before we lost him, the hens were eating their own eggs as soon as they laid them. We could barely salvage a couple of eggs from them. And when hens eat their own eggs, you must expect misfortune.

The day before Little Manoli died, my aunt Thareini sent me to feed our chickens. Since my parents had gone to Rhodes we'd rather neglected them. I entered the hen coop, and what did I see? One hen trying to tread another one, and our best hen, Whitey, crowing like a cock. I threw the feed at them in a hurry and rushed to Auntie to tell her all about it.

"Holy Mother of God, that's a bad omen!" she said. "It means we'll have news of someone's death, God forbid."

And she took the censer, lit the little coals and palm leaves from Palm Sunday in it and went around censing all the icons. It was no use. Next day we heard about our Little Manoli.

After this the hens laid regularly again and didn't eat

their eggs. Neither did they behave like cocks. But my mother, who'd heard about it, came to hate them. She really detested them.

"They knew about my boy," she said, "that he would go from us, and am I now to feed 'em and give 'em water? Never! Let 'em starve to death, let the pip kill 'em."

My father tried to reason with her this way and that. She wouldn't budge.

"Let 'em die, the witches!"

"Then it's better we kill 'em," said Father.

So my mother killed them one by one, and first of all Whitey. And to think Whitey was our best hen. I kept my distance when she cut their throats, because I couldn't bear the blood. But I could hear Mother as she reminded every hen she killed of how good they'd had it with her.

"You too, slut, who I was proud of..."

"And you, you slut, who were my favourite..."

And for as long as the hen went on cackling for the last time, Mother mumbled, "You knew it, you witch, you knew it. You knew it and didn't tell me. Eat the dust now, you hateful vampire you."

And she didn't let any of their meat pass her lips.

No smells come from the flat of the gentleman called Aleko. It seems they're still asleep.

I go up to the broad stairs of the entrance hall. Through the first door on the left comes the voice of the popular singer Parios. I can recognise his voice a mile away. He's singing, "Love me", Sotiria's favourite song. I prefer the voice of the woman singer Alexiou, actually. Sotiria has even got her own record player. Her older brother, the seaman, has brought it for her. He also gave her foreign records with it, Brazilian tangos, she says, and she showed us how to dance them. Poppycock, she doesn't know a thing; she just makes out as if she knows. Her sister, the one who likes the gendarmes, bought two records of Parios and one of Alexiou. "Parios," she says, "is absolutely the best ever."

Behind the door on the right a baby is crying its head off. What on earth is that mother doing?

There are two more doors at the back. Everything's quiet there, no voices, no smells. I go up to the first floor. Some lady's talking in a loud voice behind one of the doors:

"And tell 'er," she yells, "not to try doublecrossing me if she knows who she's dealing with. Because then *I'll* wash her dirty linen in public, and even Niagara Falls won't be enough for that! D'you hear? That's what you tell 'er! Tell 'er, Tassia won't have anyone over 'er 'ead. And if she thinks she's somebody, she's very much mistaken. The woman who can put somethin' over on Tassia's yet to be born. That's what you go tell 'er!"

I hurry past. That Tassia gives me the jitters. Just imagine she opens her door and sees me standing there. At Maria's door I stand on tiptoe and ring the bell. Maria comes to the door with a towel wrapped round her head. She's just washed her hair.

"It's only on Sundays, when the children are away, we have some peace to wash and tidy up," Maria says.

The door to the parlour is closed today. The passage is dark.

"We're sitting in here," she says and leads me into the bedroom. Kyriako, her husband, is wearing the

92

same dressing-gown. He's sitting on the double bed reading the newspaper. He's spread the paper all over the bed. Next to him, taking up a tiny bit of the bed, Maria's knitting something. At one side of the bed there's a bedside table with a large radio on it. The telephone's on top of the radio. On the other side of the bed there's a low table. Kyriako keeps his worry beads and a shoe horn on it. My Uncle Sotiri has a shoe horn like that. Poor man, he's got a bunyon on his right foot that gives him lots of trouble. In the room there's also a child's bed and a wardrobe. The furniture takes up all the space. It's very crowded; there's barely room to move about.

I sit on a chair next to the child's bed. Nobody says anything. I look through the window and see there's a balcony. It's got a railing covered over with chicken wire. But there are no chickens, or are there?

"Maria, have you got chickens?" I ask.

"Chickens?" Maria says and laughs. "Where did you get that idea, dear child?"

I'm embarrassed because she laughed. I wish I'd kept my mouth shut.

"Because of the chicken wire, I mean..."

"Ah, that's for the children, so they won't climb on the railing and fall off the balcony."

So it's chicken wire for the children! Again nobody speaks. Kyriako turns a page in his newspaper. He must have read something that burned him up, because he says: "Oh, go to hell, you bastards, you're putting something over on us."

Maria's knitting something blue. I wonder what it's meant to be and for whom.

The balcony looks on a narrow little street. On the corner there's a pile of rubbish. A grey cat has torn a hole into a rubbish bag and is stuffing itself like nobody's business. There's no one in the street, and it's cold too. Maria has some sort of flowers on the balcony. They look weak and scawny.

I'd better go back downstairs. It looks as though they're bored with me.

"I'm going downstairs," I say, "we have to go to Noufri's."

I say this, so they don't think I'm snubbing them or don't enjoy their company.

"Regards," says Maria. "Tell Noufri to give me a ring. Here, take our number." She writes it on a scrap of paper and gives it to me.

I go back down. I can smell Mother's cooking already. I wonder whether she had any cinnamon and cloves to put in the sauce. Well, she'll have managed somehow.

She's sitting at the bedroom window knitting a white vest for my father. She's brought it half-knitted from Symi. From time to time her mind seems to wander and she looks up gazing through the window. What's there for her to look at? Two metres across there's a blank wall. In our house on Symi maybe we hadn't got a bathroom, but we had fresh air. We lived high up on the hill, and from the bedroom window you could see first the nearby houses, then Myloi, Yalos, Pedi, Analepsi, and Nimos. You could even see as far as the Turkish coast from our bedroom window.

"Where's Father?" I ask.

"He's in the bathroom shaving," says Mother.

On Symi we had a little mirror hanging beside the

washstand. That's where Father shaved, and that's where we combed our hair too. It was outdoors. In winter we put a piece of corrugated roofing over it to keep the rain out. We filled the little water tank of the washstand with cistern water. The tank had a picture painted on it. I still have it clear before my eyes: two trees made with paint sprinkled in two shades of green, and five black and white sheep with some flowers beyond.

"Go ahead, set the table," says Mother. "I'll drain the spaghetti so we can eat."

I wipe the green formica top of Stavro's table. I lay out forks, the bread knife, bread. We still have some of Mother's home-made loaf.

We were still eating when the doorbell rang. Father went to the door. It was Charilaos, Eleni's husband, Maria's son-in-law. He said he'd got some business on a ship at Perama, and if we liked he could take us there in his car to save us bother. He was going in half an hour. Did we think we could make it?

"Sure, sure," Father said, "and many thanks."

Charilaos said he'd be coming for us in half an hour then.

"There you are," said Father. "So we'll be driven to Noufri's in style after all." We hurried with the rest of the meal. Mother and I washed up and she got dressed. Then we sat waiting for Charilaos.

Well, I do and I don't want to go to Noufri's. Still, I'm curious to see what his house in Athens is like. They keep their Symi house shut. It was an unlucky house too, because that's where Noufri's wife disappeared

95

from one fine day. They searched everywhere, but she was nowhere to be found. Neither did the sea wash up a body. Some said she'd run away with a soldier who'd been discharged at that time. Well, she hadn't had a good time of it with Noufri. He used to beat her up too. Some say she went into a convent, which is quite likely. But she left three daughters behind with Noufri. They must've been twelve to fifteen-years-old then and quite good-looking. But the older they got, the more jealous they became of each other. The marriage proposals came to nothing. They ruined each other's chances every time. It was a real shame. Then these other things started.

First they became hypochondriacs. They made you wash your hands when you went into their house. Then, after you left, they sprinkled methylated spirit on the chair you'd sat on and wiped it with chlorine. What man would consider marrying them after that? So they became more and more old-maidish and never married. But the worst was still to come, especially with the middle one. She wouldn't even go out of the house any more. She was afraid someone might touch her and contaminate her. And then that other thing happened to her. My mother thinks I don't know it, but Sotiria's sister's told me. One fine day, they say, as she was sitting there, she started hitting her pussy saying, "There, you're to blame for everything."

Because of all the gossip going on about his family, Noufri saw no other way out but to take his daughters and leave the island. Our fellow-islanders who live in Piraeus say Noufri is managing fine now. He's doing some kind of work in the shipyards. His youngest daughter's working too, and they're coping. So, on the one hand I want to go and see what these women are like now, and on the other I don't really want to, because I'm scared of them.

The doorbell rings. It's Kyriako Junior. He says his father is waiting for us. We lock up and walk out into the street. The north wind is blowing bitterly cold.

Charilaos is driving a yellow car. He opens the door and pushes the front seat forward. My mother, me, and Kyriako Junior climb in that way and sit in the back. Father sits in front and we're off.

Now this little devil, what did he need to sit next to me for? As soon as I try to look out of the window, he puts his head in the way. When I lean back, he leans back too. The little rascal's doing it on purpose. I can see it in the twinkle in his eye. He's making fun of me. I poke him in the ribs with my elbow. He hits back. All this is done under cover, of course, and without a word. But his father gets wind of something, because he says:

"Hey, what did I tell you before we left? Have you forgotten?"

"She started it," Kyriako says.

"Yea, sure, as if I didn't know you," says Charilaos and goes on talking to Father.

"Have you got any toys?" Kyriako asks. I look straight ahead without replying. "I've got Dinky-Toys, cranes, cars, and an electric train."

I refuse to take any notice. But what toys the rascal has! Poppycock, he's lying. An electric train indeed!

"Astradeni, you must come and play with Kyriako one of these days," says Charilaos. It seems he can both drive and listen to what we're saying. I nod. Does that

97

mean he's really got all those toys?

"She'll break them," Kyriako says, "and besides, she's a girl." Ah, but now I can't bear it any longer.

"And what's wrong with girls, if you please?" I ask.

"They've no idea how to play," says he, all superior.

That's a lot of rubbish, I feel like crying out, but I keep my cool, seeing his father's every bit of all right.

"... unemployment. Ships are tied up," Charilaos is now telling Father, "And no jobs in the shipyards either, unless you're a skilled worker. But even for them there's nothing going these days."

My mother has turned her head so as to have the air blow straight in her face. She must be nervous, because she keeps twisting the corners of her scarf between her fingers.

"Is it a long way still?" I ask.

Charilaos glances at the slip of paper with Noufri's address and says,

"Another ten minutes, about."

"You'll have Miss Maria for a teacher," Kyriako tells me.

"How d'ye know?" I ask him.

"It's the one my cousin George has who's in the fifth. She's a dragon. When she's talking she doesn't want a peep out of anyone. George is always on detention with his dictation. He has to write it five, ten times. He sits in during breaks."

"That's your cousin's fault, not the teacher's," I tell him. They all burst out laughing, except Kyriako. "I'll tell him that," he whispers, "and you'll have something coming to you."

To hell with you and your cousin. As if you're not quite a handful by yourself, you have to drag in that cousin as well. Well, disasters never come singly, as my aunt Thareini says.

"I'm letting you off here," says Charilaos stopping the car. "Just go straight on, and when you come to that delicatessen over there ask where Antheon Street is."

The street isn't very wide, and it's got narrow pavements too. The houses are small, narrow that is, but they've got two or three floors and aluminium door and window frames. It seems the Archaeological Service allows it here, so these houses aren't under "Preservation Order". In an open door a woman's feeding a small child.

"Look," she says pointing to my mother, "that lady's a nurse, she's come for the injection. You'll give him an injection with a long needle, won't you, if he doesn't eat his dinner." She nods to us while stuffing food into the boy's mouth.

We walk toward the delicatessen where we'll ask for directions. Suddenly a door opens, and a half-dressed woman rushes out. She's even putting on her other shoe after she's in the street. She bumps into my mother. Before we can figure out what's going on, the door opens again and a man in vest and pyjama trousers comes out.

"To hell with ya!" he shouts to the woman running away. "D'ya hear? Go to hell, you filthy bitch! I'll make ya the laughing stock of the whole neighbourhood. Listen, all of ya, she got 'erself a lover!" He's shouting at the top of his voice. "I beat 'er up good and proper, and I'm throwin' 'er out as I took 'er in, with just the clothes on 'er back."

While he's shouting the curtains in the windows move, which means people are at home, but no-one comes out. There's only a child crying, sitting in the

100

door the man and woman have come out of.

"Keep going," says Father, and we move on.

Boy, oh boy, what goings-on! Fancy him calling her such names within hearing of the whole neighbourhood, of her child, of strangers! But her too, to have a lover, a married woman! I wonder, is Perama a part of Athens too? I better ask Father.

"Father, this Perama, is it part of Athens?"

"Eh, sure enough. As things look, not only Perama and Piraeus, but all of Greece is going to be part of Athens. Why're you asking?"

"Just because."

We've got to the delicatessen. It's a teeny-weeny shop selling milk and yoghurt. But it's also got crackers, salt, tinned tomatoes, Turkish delight, coffee. Everything's piled up all around, and there's a large fridge with beer, wines, yoghurt. There's a gendarmerie calendar too above a picture of Christ.

About half a dozen men are sitting at the two tables in the shop watching TV. Two young men are drinking beer watching the TV show and laughing. Three little old men are sitting close together with eyes fixed on the screen. They don't seem to hear the laughter of the young men or anything else. They're just sitting there watching without a word. It's a Greek film they're showing.

"Look, now he's going to slap her," says an old man with a twinkle in his eye. Sure enough, that fat gentleman with the moustache, the one playing the father, gives his daughter such a slap, it must've reddened her cheek.

101

"There, now she's going to cry," says the old man again. And sure enough, the girl starts crying. Wait a minute, no, she's faking it, because at the same time she's looking sideways at the fatty with the moustache to see whether he sees her crying, and she goes on sobbing and shaking her head in misery.

"We're looking for Noufri's house," says Father in a loud voice, so he can be heard. They all look up for a second, then go back to watching the TV screen.

"It's the green house up the street," a fat man says. He seems to be the shopkeeper, 'cause he's serving tea in a glass. We leave the shop. I wish I could see how the film goes on.

We walk past two or three houses, and then we see it. It's got a railing round the front yard and a low iron gate, all painted green.

We walk into the yard. On the left there's a small kitchen. It's separate from the rest of the house... A kind of curtain hanging in the door opening is lifted and Noufri's two older daughters appear.

They're wearing summer shoes, no stockings, and their toenails are pitch black. Their arms are covered with soap suds to the elbow, and they're holding them up. Their hair is almost white, unkempt and sticking out around their heads. Their eyes — I'll never forget their eyes — wild, half-shut, staring at us. Their clothes are hanging on them dirty and crumpled. They're stinking from afar.

"Hello," says Father.

"Good afternoon," Mother and I say together.

"Good to see you," they say with one voice. "We're

not shaking hands because of the soap suds."

They say it as though they've learned the line by heart. The soap suds drip from their elbows on the cement floor of the yard making rows of spots and bubbles.

The house door opens and Noufri appears.

"Well-met, *koumbaro!*" he says. "Come right in." We enter a room. It's painted green, an ugly green. There's a couch, a chest of drawers and a cupboard taking up all the space.

"This way," says Noufri. "We'll go into the other room where the ole lady is."

A short while ago, his mother Evdokia came to stay with Noufri in Athens too. She's eighty but in good shape.

We enter another room. This one's painted pink. The old woman's lying in a double bed. I don't know whether she was beautiful in her youth. They say she was, but now she certainly isn't. She's all of a piece; you can't even make out her neck. She shakes hands and her hand's sweaty, though it's only March. I wipe my hand discreetly on my skirt after the handshake.

Evdokia is glad to see us. Her small dark eyes are smiling. But in a little while she starts crying. Who knows what memories have come back to her, of the island, of her younger days when she was beautiful?

"Oh come on, not that again," Noufri says irritated. "These people aren't in the mood for tears."

The bed stands against a wall with a wall-hanging, a heavy cloth with a fringe and a picture woven in it. It shows Christ blessing the multitude. He's standing near some palms with His hand raised in blessing. The people standing or kneeling before Him are looking at Christ. It says in beautiful lettering, "Christ at Emmaus".

103

The TV on a chest of drawers is still showing the Greek picture. Now the girl, looking angry, is driving a car.

Noufri gives us chairs to sit on. Then I notice a camp bed under a window with the shutters closed. Someone's asleep there. Neither the talk, nor the TV seem to wake him up. He has an army blanket pulled over his head and couldn't care less. Noufri says:

"Shall I make you some coffee, *koumbaro*?"

"No need to go to the trouble," Father says.

"As you like," says Noufri and sits down. "When there's no woman in the house... Well, the two older ones, see... never mind, and the old lady in bed..."

Evdokia sniffs and moves in bed. She must be naked under the bedclothes, because her thigh shows for a moment snow-white and fat.

"... And it's O.K. when I'm here," Noufri continues, "but I have to go out on business, and the youngest one, what d'you expect, she comes home from work dead beat. Look at 'er now, sleeping like nobody's business." So it's the youngest daughter sleeping on the camp bed. Youngest after a fashion, that is, she must be nearly thirty-five by now.

"Has she got a good job?" Father asks.

"Hmm," Evdokia shakes her head and starts crying again.

"Are you gonna cut it out at last?" Noufri bristles. "Of course she's got a good job, and the pay's very good. She sings at a night club. Lemme show you this picture; she brought it just yesterday."

He gets up to fetch the photo. It shows a young woman laughing. At her feet are a whole lot of broken plates.

"They break the plates by the dozen for her sake," says Noufri proudly.

The two older daughters come in with the soap suds still on their arms. As soon as they see the picture, they start screeching and screaming, "She's a whore, she's a whore!" Noufri gets up furious,

"Get out of here, or it'll be your last hour, you vampires. If it weren't for her, where would your next meal come from? Back to the kitchen with you. Go on, scram!"

Evdokia is whimpering in bed shaking her head to and fro. The blanket on the camp bed stirs and the youngest daughter grumbles, "Can't one even get some decent sleep in here? Shut up!"

"Let's go next door," says Noufri. "One can't even talk in this house, my God!"

Mother and I exchange glances. I'm flabbergasted. I wish we could get out of this house this very minute.

We take our chairs to the next room and sit down. The picture continues on the TV, except now I can listen but can't see anything. My hands are frozen, not because of the cold, but because I'm scared of fights.

"Well, *koumbaro*," says Father, "how do things look, as far as jobs go, I mean?" I'd say Father is shocked. He must've taken one look at us too and decided the sooner we get this over with and get out of here, the better.

"I've already told you," says Noufri, "and I'll say it again, there *is* work..."

"But Charilaos, you know, Maria's son-in-law, says there's unemployment and..."

"Never mind, he doesn't know. There's jobs, and good ones, for them that's smart. It's a good set-up, goin' like clockwork, and I can use you."

"What's there for me?" Father asks hopefully.

Good for Noufri, I say to myself. It's true what they

105

say, that he's fallen on his feet in Athens. There you are, he's got his own business too and tells Father, "I can use you!"

"Well now, this is what it amounts to. We get diesel oil out of the ships and sell it to households. There's lots of us who're party to the operation, watchmen, mechanics, three-wheeler drivers. So it works both ways, people get to buy cheaper diesel oil, and we get a good cut out of it. Your job's a cinch. You just load the machines, the three-wheelers, with canisters you pick up in the sheds, and that's all. Four hundred a day plus fares. What d'you say?"

I look at Mother, but she's looking at Father. Her hand smoothes her skirt over and over again nervously. Father takes long to reply.

"Haven't you got anything else in mind?" he says at last without looking at Noufri.

"There's nothing else. Unemployment's high. Haven't you seen all those ships tied up? And what's wrong with this job then? Don't you like it?" Noufri sounds offended.

"Nothing... nothing's wrong with it," Father hastens to say. "Only, well, I'd thought of something more permanent, more stable like..."

"Well, think about it then," says Noufri sluggishly, "and if you find something better, go ahead take it. I was trying to be helpful and kept this job open for you. Otherwise, there's plenty begging me for it."

"Sure, and lots of thanks," says Father getting up. "But we'd better be going now; we won't take up any more of your time."

"Give those people a piece of Turkish delight, for God's sake!" someone shouts. It must be the youngest daughter, the singer, because neither Evdokia, nor the other daughters have such deep voices. It seems she wasn't really asleep and heard everything.

Noufri gets up, opens the cupboard and takes out a box of Symi Turkish delight. He offers it to us as we're standing there, because Mother and me have also got up meanwhile.

"Look, Noufri," says Father, "I don't want you to think I don't appreciate your offer... but, see, I want something secure, with less money even, so I can have social insurance, y'understand. Thanks anyway for trusting me..."

"Never mind," says Noufri. "Do as you think best. If you find a job, go right ahead and take it."

We said goodbye to Evdokia from the door. The other women we didn't see again. The curtain in the kitchen door was down, and we went out into the street.

"Father," I started.

"Not a peep out of you now, Astradeni," says Father.

"But, Father..." I want us to talk. I want him to tell me about Noufri's job offer, about the singer-daughter and the others with the soap suds, about Evdokia, what we're going to do now that Noufri's offer has come to nothing.

"I've told you, Astradeni, leave off, not now. When we get home, we'll talk."

Something in Father's voice makes me shut up. He never refuses to talk to me. While Mother's a woman of few words, Father talks to me. If he's behaving like this now, who knows, maybe he can't quite grasp all that he's seen and heard himself. Maybe he wants to put it all in order in his mind first and then talk about it.

"Are we taking the bus?" I ask.

Charilaos is coming by between six and six-thirty,''
says Father.

It's twenty to six now. We're going to wait for him at
the bus stop.

I'd rather we were taking the bus to see how one gets
a ticket, how one sits in it, how people get on and off. I
want to see the driver, the other gentleman who sells
the tickets. In Charilaos' car, with that squirt Kyriako
there too... Why did he take that little twirp along when
he was going on business?

We walk along the same street that we'd come by.
Now it's deserted. All the people are shut up in their
houses, and it's bitter cold. We go past the house of the
man who threw out his wife; not a sign of life, total
stillness. And that other kid must've eaten his dinner.
The door of his house is shut.

How brave Father is! I know it's for Mother's sake he
pretends not to care that Noufri's job was no good. No
good is putting it mildly; it was plain stealing. What did
he mean "we get" diesel oil from the ships. It means we
steal the oil. Well, to make a thief of my father, that's
going too far! It can't be that in all of Athens there isn't
a decent job to be had for my father; it's out of the question. He'll find a job and a good one for sure. And then
he'll buy me a pair of shoes with button-down straps
across the instep for Easter.

We get to the bus stop. Two ladies are standing there
waiting. My mother keeps her eyes lowered. I know
Mother. When she's looking down it means both that
she's angry and that she wants to talk. Father lights a
cigarette. The ladies are in the middle of a conversation.

108

They're elderly, with grey hair and aren't wearing hats like the ones in church.

It's awfully cold. I stick my hands into my pockets. In one pocket, deep down, there's some rubbish, sesame seeds and rusk crumbs.

"Let him do his military service first, Evanthia, my dear, and then we'll see," says the one lady, the taller of the two. "Then, if he still wants her, and she wants him, let them get married. Because out of sight out of mind, as you know. Two years in the army, it'll do them both good! He'll mature, and as for her, well, we'll see, we'll see. His father and I are putting nothing in his way. Let him have her; it's they who'll have to live with each other, but if... There's the bus, Evanthia, watch out!"

A dark green bus comes. It stops suddenly, lets out a grim puffing noise like a monster and two doors open. Nobody gets off. Only the two ladies hurry to get on. The bus starts before the ladies have a chance to sit down, and they're thrown backwards. It's too funny. One grabs the other, and together they fall against some other people.

I'm amazed at all the things man has thought up and invented. He's made buses that can take, who knows, over a hundred people and can transport them from one end of Athens to the other, whereas Irene's donkey could only carry one person at a time. Yea, but Irene's donkey could find the way by himself. You loaded him with, say, barley at Saint Constantine's and gave him a slap on his bottom, and off he went knowing exactly where he was to go to. He went to the village, to Irene's house, so that Michali could unload him. That was a fantastic donkey!

One day they loaded him with bags of cement. They tied them on either side of him and on top of his saddle. He was overloaded. He was to carry them from the village to Saint Constantine's uphill all the way. It wasn't funny.

I was going that way too to see Grandma Eleni who lived in Kalyvato. I was taking her olives and sesame oil, because the 15th of August fast was starting. On the way, near Vigli, I saw Irene's donkey trotting ahead, carrying the cement. Let's see, I thought, how he'll find the way by himself, because at that point there are three roads branching off. You must take the upper road going to Panormitis in order to get to Saint Constantine's. The lower road goes to Saint Michael's. It's where the Archangel put his foot down and left a complete footmark in the rock. It's where he stopped to wash his face in the trough that's carved in the rock, and where he sat in the stone armchair to rest. How big the Archangel must be! His foot is five times larger than mine. Three kids fit in his chair, blessed be his name. A bit further is Kalafatina's Bottom. This Kalafatina, she sat on a rocky seat too, and the stone cracked under her weight! Her enormous bottom has left a mark so-o big in the stone! Well, never mind.

Irene's donkey took the right road, the upper one. I was walking beside him looking at him. He was looking at me too.

"D'you mind," I say, "if I rest my basket on your back?"

"And why should you mind," I say again. "With such

110

a heavy load you're carrying, you might as well add my little basket to it.''

He kept looking at me, then twitched one ear, as if to say, ''All right!'' I perched my basket on his back and we walked on together.

Now no matter how many thousands of times I went on that road to Saint Constantine's, the same thing always happened to me. I started talking aloud, although I was by myself. You see, I don't know quite how to say it, but one time I fancied I was a deer, like those in the Natural History book, and I was running. Another time I was a princess who'd fled to the mountains to escape the Turks and the pirates.

''Today I'm going to be a fairy,'' I said to Irene's donkey, ''and you're going to be Prince Charming. A bad witch has turned you into a donkey, and I'm the only person who can make you human again, because I'm a good fairy. Only you must do whatever I tell you. That's why I've made you carry my basket.''

Irene's donkey got the point, I'm sure. He was walking very slowly, as though he were very depressed about being a prince turned donkey. I knew, of course, he was going slowly because of the heavy load, but, as I said, we were playing the prince and the fairy.

We arrived at the Myrtles and I stopped. I broke a myrtle twig off and put it in my hair speaking the verses we always speak when we come to that spot.

> When passing by a myrtle
> Don't fail a twig to break
> For if you don't, your true love
> Vile death from you will take.

The donkey stopped and wouldn't go on. He fixed huge

111

pleading eyes on me. Could it be, I thought, he wants some myrtle too, so he doesn't lose his true love? I broke off a twig and fastened it between his ears. And the rascal started walking at once! Well, there was no doubt he'd taken the game very seriously.

We walked past Saint Catherine's. When Kalyvatos and Saint Constantine's appeared in the distance, I took hold of my basket and gave the donkey a shove.

"Giddyup!" I said. "See that you hurry to Irene who's waiting for you. And woe to you if you breathe a word to anyone about fairies and princes!"

With his head hanging low he started uphill. He was sad. There's not many who'd bother to play with a beast and make a prince of him for a little while, even if it's just an enchanted prince. A great little donkey he was, God bless him.

Now how come I remembered Irene's donkey? Here my father's just lost a job and I'm thinking of fairies, donkeys and princes. Really, I can't be quite right in the head!

I think I see a yellow car coming. Sure enough it's Charilaos. He stops and we get into the car. We sit as before. I've decided I'm not going to speak to Junior. And if he talks to me I'll pretend I don't hear him or can't understand him. He's just sitting there reading a magazine. I wonder what sort of magazine it is. Let's have a look. Hmm, it's not *Mickey Mouse*, it says *Popeye.* The little monster! As soon as he realizes I'm looking he shifts in his seat so I can't see.

It's almost dark now. We drive past some places with lots of lights. We must be next to a river.

Charilaos asks Father about Noufri's job offer. Father says it won't do for the moment. That's what he said, "for the moment". He spoke so between his teeth that even Charilaos, who's a stranger, got wind of something, for he said:

"Take care you don't get mixed up in some kind of dirty business. These characters have turned into jackals. They do anything you can think of. They supply coloured crews illegally, make deals with the stewards and sneak in rotten meat and tinned food for the crews, to say nothing of the whiskey, the foreign cigarettes, the colour TVs."

"Yea, sure," says Father, "I understand." The car stops. There are plenty of cars ahead of us and more cars behind.

"This is Fokionos Negri Street," Kyriako says. Big deal, who cares. But what women, by George! Real fashion models! Where do so many and such good-looking women come from? And the clothes! One is even wearing something that looks like bloomers! And someone who looks like a man is wearing one earring; *one* earring! They're sitting at these cafés full of lights, red chairs, shiny tabletops. The car starts again, but I turn around and keep looking, looking. Presently we turn into a side street and have arrived at our place.

We get out of the car and go home. We've hardly taken our coats off when the bell rings. It's Maria.

"Why don't you come on upstairs," she says. "You don't want to sit here all by yourselves. Come up for a little chat, to reminisce about Symi."

My mother gives her a look that's a sort of signal. I've

noticed that grown-up women, like my mother and Maria, can look at each other and give a signal. They may half-close their eyes or cock their head ever so slightly or purse their lips. All this is done so discreetly, that nobody else notices anything. But *they've* passed on a message to each other. Just like now with my mother and Maria. Without a word they've said everything about the job, Father, his worries. Men don't know how to do this.

We go up using the stairs. Maria won't go into a lift either. She says she suffers from claustrophobia; she's afraid of confined spaces. She says she hasn't even been to the pictures for twenty years. She won't get on a bus, won't go to the theatre, even to the shops in downtown Athens. And if she rides in a car, her son-in-law's for instance, she must sit next to the driver beside the door. That's another funny thing I've never heard of. Well, all I can say is, give me a chance to go to the pictures or the theatre, and I betcha nothing like that happens to me.

Kyriako Senior's wearing his dressing-gown, but he's not watching TV. He's sitting in his armchair playing with his worry beads.

We sit on the sofa. Maria offers us roasted chick-peas and raisins. She offers Father a glass of brandy. Father's not talking. They exchange knowing glances again, Mother and Maria, and they look at me too.

"Astradeni," says Maria, "d'you want me to give you some of Kyriako's toys to play with?" I nod. I know they want to be rid of me, to talk without me listening. As if I can't hear everything from the room next door. Anyway, I do want to play with Kyriako's toys.

Maria takes me to the bedroom. She takes a small wooden slab out of the cupboard. On closer look I see it

114

isn't just a wooden slab. It's a thickish flat piece of wood with some pictures fitted in it, a lorry, a tiny car, and some other things. Maria shakes the thing and the pictures fall out of their places.

"Now find the places they fit into again," she says, leaving the room.

Big deal! I take the lorry and put it in the upper left corner, where I can see its shape perfectly well. Then come the red car, the blue one, the yellow one. No, the yellow one doesn't fit here, it fits in the next space. Then comes the other little lorry with the stripes — finished! That was a game for little kids. What now? Go next door where they want to talk? It isn't right. I'll sit still as though I'm at the game and listen to their talk.

"Listen, Nicola," it's Kyriako Senior speaking, "I spent all my years, eighteen to be precise, at sea. But me too, I wanted to stay at home with the family. So I said no to the big wages and the big voyages. Maria went to work too, and we managed."

"They were hard years," Maria pipes in, "but the girls had their father to stand by them."

"How did you cope?" Father asks.

"I worked on a yacht, the DAPHNE. It was small, an old mine sweeper, and it had a hard time in storms, because it was flat-bottomed. It had been converted for the tourists. It was hired out to Americans, Germans, French — but mostly Americans. The cruises started, depending, sometimes in April, sometimes May, and stopped in September. Every ten days or so we touched Piraeus. The group we had on board left, and we took on a new lot. We sailed round here, just the islands. We got as far as Italy and Turkey a couple of times, but mainly it was the Cyclades, Crete, the Dodecanese. The meals

115

were O.K. When the tourists left, they tipped the crew. With salary plus tips we managed pretty good."

"You see," says Maria, "Kyriako worked in the winter too, when the boats were tied up."

"Maintenance work on the engines," Kyriakos explains. There's silence for a while.

"It wasn't bad at all," says Kyriako, as if he'd thought deeply before saying it.

"It'd be a godsend if Nicola could find such a job," says Maria, and goes on before Mother or Father can say anything, "You see, he can ring you from the islands and be home every fortnight. And in winter, with the storms, he stays home."

"Well, we've put the sea out of the question," says Father.

"I don't know," says Kyriako. "That's your business. But should you decide otherwise, I can put in a good word for you with Captain Andreas. You can sail as second engineer, or boatswain. What sort of papers have you got?"

"Third engineer and diesel," Father says.

"Just right," says Kyriako. "Only don't take forever to make up your mind. In a week or so they'll be hiring crews."

"Well, we thought he should stay on land," my mother says. "We're stangers here. If Nicola goes, us two women will be left all alone."

Mother's afraid of being alone. Whenever Father was away for several days she was all nerves, like a caged animal. And she asked some boy, Dino or Michalio, to come stay with us on those nights. If I'm about to be

116

afraid of the bogeyman or the witch, I say a "Jesus Christ conquers", and my fear goes away. As for elves and fairies, I'm not scared of them at all. Not only that, I wish I could run into them and get to know them.

We spent a few days at the Great Monastery of Our Saviour once. Father had some business there, and we stayed in a small cell of a place. It was very pleasant. I made a good friend there too, Irene. She was very pretty, prettier than me. She had blond hair she wore in braids and strange slanted eyes, a little like Chinese eyes. She had pierced ears too and wore circle earrings. We played house together. We made dolls out of plastic bottles with stuffed cloth heads. We embroidered eyes and mouths and stitched hair on them and played.

It was the first week in August, days full of magic we call *drimes.* For six days you may not wash clothes or swim in the sea. And if you water the garden in the evening, your vegetables'll dry up. It's the water fairies that are responsible for all this. And what the weather's like during those days, that's what it'll be for the whole year. It was good weather on the 1st of August, so January and February were going to be mild. On the 2nd of August it turned cloudy and strangely cool for summer, so the grown-ups said March would be freezing and April cool. On the 3rd, 4th and 5th it was hot, so from May on till October it would be hot. On the 6th of August it was close, hot and humid with mist in the morning. That day Irene and me had an idea.

"Say, shall we play fairies?"

"Let's!"

We took our bread and cheese along and said we were

117

going to light the oil lamps at the Kourkouniotis chapel. When we got to the copse, we let our hair down, took our shoes off and started dancing. We'd agreed on the way to be dumb and communicate only with gestures and signs. Inwardly we were to pray very earnestly that we might get to see the water fairies, because there are brooks in the copse.

We danced and danced, we made some magic signs, but nothing happened. No elf, no fairy showed up, who knows why. So then we thought we'd eat our bread and cheese. We were still barefoot and with our hair down. There were some nice flat stones under the pines, and there we sat down to eat. There was a circle of whitewashed stones around us. We sat in the middle of the circle and ate in silence as agreed. It was cool and pleasant.

Irene was in a playful mood, rocking to and fro on her stone that wasn't sitting flat on the ground. Suddenly the stone tilted and Irene fell over. She didn't even cry "Ouch!", just as we'd agreed!

Then we saw this small bunch of reeds under the stone. There were five pieces stuck together, each one shorter than the one before it, like a staircase. They also had holes neatly cut into them. It was a flute like the ones the shepherds play, except it had five reed pipes. "Shall I blow on it?" I motioned to Irene, seeing as we hadn't agreed not to play a reed pipe, only not to talk. "Yes," she motioned back.

I know how to play the single flute that my cousin Vassili's taught me. I started blowing on the five reeds. My goodness me, what a beautiful sound came out! Like a light breeze in the trees. Then something seemed to urge me to pipe faster and faster. Some goats grazing nearby were scared and scampered off as if in a panic. But Irene too must've been scared, because she made signs to me to stop. But I was fascinated by the sounds I was making and kept blowing on the flute.

Irene started running toward the monastery. I couldn't call out to her, 'cause we'd agreed to be dumb. Neither did I really want to. I just wanted to go on blowing on the flute.

When I'd had enough of playing the flute, I put it back in its place for the shepherd who'd hidden it there to find again. It was ever so still; not a leaf stirred. I lay down and watched the pine needles that were making all sorts of patterns above my head. It was as if the pines were breathing out the scent of resin.

It was the smell, that goat smell, not any sound I heard that made me turn my head and look. A huge billygoat was standing behind some rocks, staring at me. He was enormous. I could just see his head and his hind legs, because the rock hid his body. I never thought a billygoat could have such a shaggy head. He stared at me without moving at all. But there was something in his stare I didn't like. Still, I didn't want to run away either. I just sat there and stared back. I wondered what he was going to do. He couldn't stand there so still forever, he was bound to go. But he didn't go. He just kept staring at me. And I got really scared when he raised his head and let out a loud "Mmmm..." It's still ringing in my ears and it sounded like a human voice.

By the time I got back to the monastery I'd braided my hair and put on my shoes. I asked who the big billygoat belonged to that had scared me. I was told nobody up there owned such a billygoat. It was my imagination, they said, I must've just seen some big goat.

I asked some shepherds I knew if they could make flutes with five reed pipes, and they said, "There's no such thing."

Grandma Eleni says it's my name, Astradeni, that's to blame, because Astradeni means "the one who binds the stars".* And who other than a fairy creature can bind the stars? I don't tell anyone this, of course, because they'll say I'm "touched". But I know it's there. When this thing comes over me like a tremour, like a sweet faint, like fear, and I don't know why, then I'm afraid I'll hear some bad news or something bad'll happen. Like that time of the big earthquake that came from the Nisyros volcano. Two days before something kept bothering me. I couldn't relax, everything annoyed me. I wanted to get away from Symi but didn't know where to go.

Then again, when Pelagia's ring with the green stone was lost, something told me, "Look behind the water barrel," and I found it. Everyone was amazed. And once, when the women were talking about Anitsa, saying, "Well, it's all over with her, she's an old maid: who's going to marry her at thirty-five," I said without meaning to, it just slipped out by itself, "She's going to get married within the year." And that's exactly what happened. One of our islanders came back from Australia and married her. He was older too, of course, but he married her, *that's* what mattered.

I want to learn about magic and spells, to be able to cast out the evil eye, to break the moonspells. But I'm

* *astra*, stars; *deno*, to bind.

still too young. That's why I'm in this room. If I weren't so young, I would be sitting with the grown-ups.

What if Father doesn't find a job? But that's out of the question. There are so many people who live and work in Athens, so why shouldn't Father get a job?

I listen to the talk in the next room again. They aren't talking about anything that matters any more. Maria's asking for news of relatives and friends. Then they talk about school, my school. Maria's going to take us there tomorrow.

We're sort of glum when we get back home. I think Father was counting on the job he could get through Noufri, and he's very depressed now. Or maybe he's depressed because Noufri's changed and become — how did Charilaos put it, I liked that word — a fox, a wolf, no, a *jackal,* that's what he said, Noufri's became a jackal!

We ate without much appetite, just to eat something, like medicine you must take to get well. Not that the food didn't taste good; it was every bit of all right, and there was plenty of sauce for the spaghetti. But we'd just lost our appetite.

I fell into a deep sleep without dreams. I may have had some of course, but I don't remember them.

Today's an important day for me. I'm going to my new school, my Athens school, which I'm sure is fantastic. It simply can't be that all these kids here aren't going to super schools. After all, one doesn't live in Athens for nothing.

On Symi our school is built of dressed stone and has a red tile roof. It's also got a triangular pediment with a circle in the middle. By the gate with the wrought-iron patterns there's a carved stone that says, "31st August 1876". That's how old our school is. It's so old, it's almost lost the pebble patterns in the pavement of the yard. The children's feet wore them out over the years. So many children, so many years, the poor pebbles simply wore away and vanished.

But we've created garden plots all around the yard, and each class plants it's own plot. And because the plots are big, we divide them up among class groups. Stamatia, myself, Irene and Thareini were the third group in my class. Only it was the onions that fell to our lot. That is, Ma'am drew lots and said, "The first group will plant broad beans, the second group small lilies (the lucky ones!), the third group (that was us) onions (disgusting! We couldn't have done worse. And they don't even produce a flower). The fourth group will plant chick-peas."

But the sixth year, the older ones, had all the luck.

Tsambika's aunt, who lives in Athens, sent her a packet of seeds for flowers called "sweet peas". She brought some to school and sowed them on the very edge of the plot. In the spring they produced the most incredible flowers in all sorts of colours, and we were all crazy about them. We gathered the seed (it looked like peas) and this year we sowed them all around the garden.

They'll blossom in May but I won't get to see them, seeing I'm now living in Athens. Oh heck! What's come over me. After all, I'm not going to cry just 'cause I won't see the school sweet peas in blossom. That would be the end! I bet there'll be thousands of flowers at the Athens school. They're bound to have the most beautiful and the rarest ones.

Mother combs my hair: the parting in the middle and two identical braids with red clips at the tips. My school smock is washed and ironed (when did she iron it without me noticing?) and the collar in place. My school bag, the crisps, are all ready. My bag is red, white and blue. White is the pocket on the front. Maria, who now lives above us on the second floor, had sent it to me from Athens. All the girls were green with envy. On that white pocket there's a girl and a boy kissing. They're kissing, because the boy's a seaman who's come back from abroad and found his fiancée again. No one's told me this; I've just thought it up myself.

Father searches his pockets to make sure he's got the paper from the Symi school. Maria's late, and I'm so anxious. Suppose I get that dragonish teacher. Maria rings our bell three times. Mother makes the sign of the cross over my head and kisses me.

Maria's waiting for us at the door. She says, "Oho, that's quite a school girl!" and we're on our way. She says she's coming with us as a witness that we really live at this address. Because, she says, many lie about living in this neighbourhood in order to send their children to this school. And because the school's got too many children, they have to check carefully. You take along a water, or electricity, or phone bill to prove that you're really living at the address you give.

Fancy that, they don't believe you, and you must show them papers. And because we have no papers, we'll show them Maria who's got papers and they know her. Funny business this, and complicated too. On Symi you go to school just like that, with nothing. Never mind, this is Athens.

We come to a very broad street. There's a hospital here too, a very big one. It's three floors high and all glass windows.

"Here we are," says Maria.

I'm stunned. Is it possible they lied to me about taking me to school in order to take me to a hospital? They know I'm scared of doctors and hospitals and they've tricked me this way. But then why the school smock? Could it be this isn't a hospital but really a school?

"It's very big," says Father impressed.

"Sure," says Maria, "eighteen hundred children go to school here. Three different schools are housed in this building. We must find out which school Astradeni belongs to and the times she'll be coming."

I'm speechless. Fancy eighteen hundred kids and three schools together. And how am I to know which is *my* school? How am I to tell it apart? And my class, which one'll be my class, and how am I going to find it?

124

Fancy, eighteen hundred children!

On Symi the entire school was sixty kids. And the other school at Yalos had about a hundred. There were eighteen of us in my class, and the third year, that was next door, was sixteen kids. Classes were taught by twos. The same teacher taught the third and fourth years together. While we were writing an essay, the third year took dictation. When the third year had history, we did copying of text. We sat two at a desk, one row of girls' desks, one row of boys' desks. I sat with Doukissa at the third desk. In front sat Stamatia with Irene, behind them Irene and Alemina, then me and Doukissa, and behind us Maroula and Vasoula. The boys were all sitting in the next row of desks.

What girls am I going to sit with here, I wonder.

We walk in. The whole school is painted grey. It's really like a hospital; I can't get over that idea. There's a high railing around it that gives you the feeling you're penned in. They've got a thing here in Athens about fencing kids in: chicken wire on Maria's balcony, high railings round the school. Very odd.

We cross a very big yard. Sure, it's for eighteen hundred kids after all. But where are they? I can't see a soul. We come to a passage.

''You wait here, Astradeni,'' Father says. I grab him by his trouser leg. I'm not going to be left alone here. It's full of passages and doors and eighteen hundred children. I'll get lost; I'll lose my father.

"I'm not letting go of you," I say.

"All right, you can wait outside the Head's office." The Head's office! So this is the Head's office. If I lean over a little, I can have a peep. I can see some chairs covered in leather and another door beyond.

I sit down in a hurry, 'cause a door opens somewhere. A little boy runs past me like a shot and asks, "Have you been sent out of the room?" but doesn't even stop for an answer. From somewhere I hear a lot of kids reciting in unison, "The unstressed ah" — on the "ah" they raise their voices — "on the ultimate of the imperative of verbs is lo-ong."

Father comes out of the office with Maria and a gentleman. Could that be the Head?

"Well, Astradeni," says Father, "you belong to the 26th Primary School. You'll be having morning classes from eight to one Mondays, Tuesdays and Wednesdays, and afternoon classes from two to seven Thursdays, Fridays, and Saturdays. This gentleman is the school's caretaker and he'll take you to your class. Lessons have started already. I'll come for you at one o'clock, O.K.?"

Father bends over me with his hand on my back.

"O.K.?" he says again.

Yes, I nod. He's told me everything all at once, and I'm all mixed up.

"Come along," says the gentleman called the caretaker and walks ahead. I take a few steps, then turn around and look at my father. He waves to me. Tears are coming to my eyes.

Where am I going? As long as I have my parents beside me, I'm not scared of this strange place. But now I'm on my own. It's one thing to be alone on the island, and another thing here. It's more scary here.

Well now, Mistress Astradeni, what's the idea? Are you going to burst into tears, for the new teacher to see you in such a state as to form the wrong first impression? So, pull yourself together, perk up, and follow that gentleman they call the caretaker.

126

We stop in front of a door. It has three signs on it:

26th Primary School, Class E3

30th Primary School, Class E4

31st Primary School, Class B1

O.K., then, this is my class, the E3. I must look for something to help me find it again. Well, we'll see. Now the gentleman opens the door and pushes me in gently.

First thing I see is Ma'am. I can't tell whether she's young or old. She's got her hair pulled back into a tight knot and wears glasses.

"What is it, George?"

"A new girl, Miss."

So she's "Miss", not "Ma'am". She's not married, though she's no spring chicken.

"And of all the classes they chose to send her to mine? I've already got sixty-two in here. Never mind, thank you, George."

I'm standing somewhere near the teacher's desk. I look at the classroom. It's large, yet it's full to bursting with kids. There are four rows of desks. At most of them there are three kids. And there are two more desks next to the teacher's desk.

"Find a place and sit down," says Ma'am.

Two girls are sitting at the third desk in the second row. They look likeable and I walk toward them. But by the time I've got there, they've slipped to either end of the desk and pretend not to see me. What do I do now? Do I say, "Move over"? No, I can't. I look around. They all pretend to be looking into their exercise books, but I know they're watching me. What do I do?

I heave a sigh. Further along there's another desk with a free seat. A boy and a girl are sitting there. I go over. When I get to them, they too have moved to either end of the desk. I look around, uncertain what to do. I hear some giggles. They're doing it on purpose. They don't want me to sit next to them, but why? I must have gone red as a beet. I turn and face them. I wish I could disappear into the ground. I'm just standing there with a hard lump going up and down my throat.

"Haven't you sat down yet?" asks Ma'am from her desk. What shall I say? That they're making fun of me?

"Come and sit at one of the desks along the side," she says. There are two desks placed sideways under the window. The front desk is occupied by two girls and a boy. A boy's sitting alone at the desk behind.

"Sit with George who's on detention. The rest of you can finish your dictation."

I sit down. George looks me up and down but says nothing. He isn't taking the dictation. I put my bag on the desk and wait. I don't know what I'm supposed to do, so I watch the teacher. She's wearing a grey skirt and jacket, and shoes with low heels and laces. They're grey too. She's busy with something on the desk. George sees that I'm looking at her, gives me a little shove with his knee, and then takes hold of the point of his collar giving it a good shake. I know this gesture means so much as "the teacher's a real harridan." I pretend to pay no attention and keep looking straight ahead. Come to think of it, this George could be young Kyriako's cousin. Sure he is, for he's on detention too. Except I don't know the teacher's name.

The kids seem to have finished their dictation, because some girls get up, collect the exercise books and take them over to the teacher.

"Now," she says opening a green book, "you, the new girl, stand up and tell me your name."

I stand beside my desk and say, "Astradeni Had-zipetrou."

Ma'am isn't looking at me. She's about to write my name in the book (it must be the register) but the kids start laughing, I don't know why. She raises her head, strikes the desk with a ruler and says:

"Quiet, you lot! What did you say your name was?"

"Astradeni Hadzipetrou."

"Hadzipetrou sounds right to me, but Astradeni, is that a *Christian* name?"

I nod "yes" with my head, I'm shaking. It seems she doesn't like my name.

"Do you mean to say this is the name the priest gave you at your christening?" she asks again.

"I was christened Asterope, but they call me Astradeni."

"And Asterope, is that a *Christian* name?"

"Yes, Ma'am. Our Ma'am, my teacher, I mean my old teacher, told me it's a very ancient name. It's one of the seven stars of the Pleiades."

What's come over me that I say all these things? There you are, the kids are laughing; they're laughing their heads off in fact.

"Quiet!" shouts the teacher striking the desk with her ruler again. "I know of no such name. But never mind, when's your Saint's day, so I can make sense of all this?"

"There's no Saint's day for Asterope; I've only got a birthday."

More laughter from the class. But why on earth are they laughing like this? I must try to patch it all up somehow, or else this teacher will put me on her blacklist.

"Some girls called Asterope, Ma'am, celebrate their nameday on Saint Urania's Day. But I have no nameday."

"Well then to get this over with," says Ma'am and writes "U-RA-NIA HA-DZI-PET-ROU" speaking out each syllable.

"Asterope, Ma'am!" I cry. "That's my name."

"You watch it now, because you and I won't get along if you go on like this! I'll call you Urania, which is a name in accordance with our Church, and that's that."

"But Ma'am..."

"Miss, not Ma'am. From which school have you come to us?"

"From the Chorio School on Symi."

Nothing could hold the kids any more. But what the devil, may God forgive me, have I said again to make them laugh like that?

"All right, you may sit down now. Well, let's see, all of you who are giggling. Do you know what Symi is?" asks the teacher. They all fall silent for a while. Then a girl raises her hand and says it's a town in Euboea.

"Not *Kymi* but *Symi*," says Miss sternly — I must get used to this Miss, Miss, Miss.

"Well then, tell us, Hadzipetrou, what Symi is, since the class don't know it."

"It's one of the Dodecanese islands," I say.

Then we open our reading books and talk about all the poetic elements in the assigned text. Miss asks Petropoulou, who seems to be her pet, to give me the timetable and tell me what exercise books I must keep. All this during break, of course.

In a few minutes I hear the bell ring. It's very loud. All the kids run out of the classroom. More kids from other

130

classrooms tumble down the stairs. You'd think thousands of horses are stampeding.

George is allowed no break, since he's on detention. Petropoulou and another girl come up to my desk. Petropoulou has blond hair held to one side of her head by a silver clip. Her school smock is very neatly made and has got a lace collar. She's wearing white socks and beige shoes with a strap across the instep. She looks very neat and clean. The other one must be her friend. She's chewing on a doughnut, and there's sugar stuck all around her mouth. George has covered his face with his hands as if he's sleeping, but I'm sure he's listening. Petropoulou reads out the timetable to me day by day, lesson by lesson. I'm writing it down saying yi-es, yi-es, so she can go on. At some point she stops reading.

"If you say 'yi-es' once more, I'll drop everything and go. This peasant accent of yours is getting on my nerves."

I feel a hot wave rising in my face, and my eyes grow dim. I guess I'm blushing. Good Lord, what have I done wrong again?

"What's wrong with saying yi-es? How else am I to say it?"

"Well, well, get this true native of the capital," George mumbles. "And since when, if you please, has Levadia become the capital of Greece and I didn't know it?"

"Don't think I haven't heard what you've just said," Petropoulou cries angrily. "Maybe my dad came from Levadia, but my mummy's an Athenian. Yes, indeed! And my grandpa, if you really must know, was an officer in the army."

She's really mad. She starts off on all sorts of yarns,

about her grandpa whom the King summoned to his presence and said, "Save the Fatherland from danger!", and about her mummy who's the most beautiful mummy of the whole class. Her friend keeps nodding all the while, as if to confirm it's all exactly as Petropoulou says. George pretends to be snoring very loudly, and this annoys her even more.

The more I look at her, the more I think Petropoulou's like Sotiria, except that this one is blond. She tells me what exercise books I must keep too. Most of them are the same as we had on Symi. I only need to get a GENERAL one she says.

The bell rings. The kids come in and we have Religious Instruction. I know the chapter "St Paul in Prison", as we'd already done it on Symi. We were five pages ahead in the book.

The bell rings again. This time I go out too. The yard's full of kids, really full. The big boys are playing football. The girls are walking about in groups. The youngest kids are running around like mad; they tear past you, they hide behind you.

I locate the water taps. At the other end of the yard, on the right, there's a long trough with many taps. Even so you must queue up to get a drink of water, that's how many kids there are. As I'm standing there behind a little girl, I hear someone say, "Asteria's come to have a drink too," and the other girls giggle at the joke. I don't care, let 'em say whatever they like. Let 'em laugh all they want. I'm not even goin' to turn around and look. I don't know who she is; I don't want to know. I have a drink of water and walk on alone, just like that. Then I see a little glass house in the middle of the yard. The kids come up to the open window and buy things from a man. And what all don't they buy! Chips, crisps, chocolates, waffles, orange drinks, sweets, chewing gum. Where on earth do they get all the money? They buy two packets at a time; the school must be full of rich kids.

The bell rings. It's very loud and can be heard coming from all directions. We stand in line. I haven't lost sight of Petropoulou. Wherever she went, I went. So I found my class and stood at the end of the line.

We march to the classroom to have a history lesson. We were eight chapters ahead of them on Symi.

Just before school's out, Miss says we're to bring fifty drachmas tomorrow. On Saturday we're going to the Museum. A museum in Athens! Well, sure we've got a museum on Symi, but the Athens Museum must be something fantastic!

On Symi they tried to collect everything old that was still around in the houses: island dress, lace, crochet work, painted or carved chests, weapons, bracelets, coins, silk embroideries, copper coffee pots. They added all the ancient things and the old icons and so put our museum together. It was very neat. For a building they took the Hadziagapitos house up at Chorio and renovated it.

In the courtyard, among the pots of marigolds and basil, they set up some big ancient pieces of marble. In one room they have ancient potsherds on display. In other rooms are the icons and the weapons.

But the best job was done in the big room. The walls are still covered with the pictures that were originally painted on them: little angels, pink and green ribbons, flowers, fruit. The ceiling is painted all over too. Between the mirror and the chests they've set up big dolls wearing our old island dress, the everyday one, as well as the fur-trimmed one. They've got a male doll too in the breeches of old times. The first time I went in, I thought the dolls were alive. When I realized they were dummies I was disappointed. Then I imagined them talking to each other in the evenings, or on days when the museum had no visitors. They'd walk about, eat out of the soup terrines placed nearby and live a secret life of their own. Actually the one in the fur-trimmed dress was in love with the man, that's how I imagined it. But the man wanted the other one, the one in the everyday dress. Then the one in the fur-trimmed dress thought the reason for this was the moth-eaten crochet work round her scarf.

That's why in the night, and without the other two noticing, she went to the next room and stole a beautiful piece of mauve and green crochet work. So it's the one in the fur-trimmed dress that stole the crochet work and not a tourist, as the guards thought. And she wears the stolen piece when the guards are away, so they won't realize she's alive.

They could really be alive, if they wanted to, those dolls in the museum. There's everything there a household needs except food. But dolls don't need any food. And in the evening I fancy them going out into the yard and gazing through the arches at Yalos below with its electric lights and the music from the taverns and shaking their heads as if to say, "There are so many things we left too soon to see and to experience, really."

I thought too that maybe in a hundred or two hundred years me too, I might be a doll in the museum. I might be wearing my school smock or my yellow jacket with the ducklings, and my hair braided, and people would be walking past looking at me and saying, "How beautiful girls were *then*!"

I'd be hearing them, but my eyes would be staring straight ahead without moving. Yet in the evening I'd be walking with the other dolls in the yards and on the terraces gazing at Yalos from above.

What might we be seeing then, a hundred or two hundred years from now, I wonder.

I wait till the kids and the teacher have gone before I leave the classroom too. In the yard there are only a few boys now playing football. Father's standing at the gate. He asks me how I got along in the new school, and I just say, "fine", what else. Or should I tell him that the teacher will call me Urania to make a Christian of me, or that they're making fun of me and I could find no place to sit; or that "yi-es" had got on Miss Petropoulou's nerves. I only tell him I need a fifty-page exercise book and fifty drachmas, because we're going to the Museum on Saturday.

I've already finished my homework. Religious Instruction and History I only had to revise, as I'd already done it all on Symi. The rest of the homework didn't take long either. Father's gone out. He's gone to the tailor's to see about a job.

My mother's knitting at the window. I did my homework at Stavro's table with the light on. The weather's dull; it looks like rain. I've got nothing else to do. After I'd finished homework, I tidied up my exercise books. I wonder, are there no other children, except young Kyriako, living in this house? And what do they do shut up in their flats after they've done their homework?

I look at my mother knitting. Her hands move like a machine. She uses five needles passing from one to the other. In this way she knits Father's vest without seams. On Symi they suggested she should knit seamless sweaters and sell them to the tourist shops. That's how good she is. Her knitting's flawless, and she knits a pattern where the sleeve joins. She hasn't realized I've finished my homework and am looking at her. I wonder what she's thinking. Does she like Stavro's flat? What does she think of Athens where she didn't want to come to begin with?

My mother did not want us to come to Athens. She'd never left the island, except that time with our Little Manoli, and she's afraid of the big city.

136

"Here on Symi," she told Father, "there's always someone to turn to when you need help. There we'll be strangers among strangers."

But Father had made up his mind, and here we are. Now Mother'll be thinking about the lamp on Little Manoli's grave, about her flowers, her home, her sisters, her little corner with the stool where she sat knitting.

Ough, what'll I do now? My feet are going to and fro under the chair. I'll go mad. I'm suffocating, not from the heat, but from being shut up in here. Suppose I go out into the little yard.

"All right," says Mother, "only behave yourself." I take the broom and start sweeping the yard. It's ten paces long and six wide. I sweep the dust into a corner, and it reminds me of sweeping at Saint Constantine's. I had the same kind of broom on a long stick, and I swept the yard under the holm oak, while Irene Fotara was working in the kitchen.

Let's say then that this little yard is the yard at Saint Constantine's, and that the little fig tree at the end behind the drain pipe is the holm oak. The holm oak is very big, of course. It takes three men to put their arms around it. But the yard too is ten times bigger than this little courtyard, so we're all right. I must find some lime to whitewash the little yard all around and fancy I'm up there at Saint Constantine's.

I used to like it up there at Saint Constantine's. There's always a breeze, even when the village below is suffocating in the heat. And it's very quiet. You can hear the sheep bells, some bleating from time to time, and that's all.

Very occasionally a shepherd comes by for a drink of water, 'cause there's a spring at Saint Constantine's. You can't see it, but you can hear it dripping between the rocks. It's like a cave, and they've built a trough in front, where the water gathers. It's one of the few springs we've got on the island. That's why the gates of the monastery are always open and passers-by can go in and quench their thirst. When there's extra water, after it's rained a lot, it flows in a stream to water Irene's garden. She sows clover for the livestock and grows some vegetables for herself.

Irene spends six months of the year at the monastery. It's no longer a monastery really. It must be at least a hundred years since there were monks living there. We don't even know who built it or anything. The Archaeological Service came, made a list of the icons, the old Gospels, the votive offerings, the chalices, and said the chapel was Byzantine and we shouldn't whitewash its walls again. We whitewashed only the lower part of the walls, 'cause the plaster was crumbling.

This little monastery belongs to our family; we look after it, that is. There's one family responsible for every little monastery, and there are plenty of them on the island. This way they're all kept tidy and whitewashed. My great-grandma Martha happened to be living here at Saint Constantine's many years ago. She was the mother of my grandma Eleni and my great-aunt Dikissi.

Great-aunt Dikissi, Irene's mother, was a grand old lady. I can remember her very well. She died very old at ninety. Toward the end she was all mixed up about time and said she was waiting for her long-dead husband to

138

come back from Mersa Matruh, where he'd gone to dive for sponges. She confused her childhood with the present. She said it was time to make the doughnuts for the Saint's feast and to bring out and wash all the special bowls for the stuffed vine leaves. These special ceramic bowls, used for serving food to the pilgrims in the old days, had been put away in the attic. Only a few of them were still left.

Great-aunt Dikissi also sent word to the musicians. And when she'd set up the feast in her mind, she took hold of one of the special bowls, hid it behind her back and led the dance, as she'd done in her youth. She was the greatest dancer at Saint Constantine's. The musicians were supposed to be sitting by the old monk's cell. She came out of the side of the chapel, and took a few steps, her left arm stretched out, but bent a little coyly, her right hand holding the bowl behind her back. She moved with tiny steps for such a big woman, till she got to the arches, where she fancied the crowd was sitting, and... CRASH! She smashed the bowl with a single movement in the middle of the yard.

It was only Auntie Dikissi who saw the yard full of people. She went on with her dance listening to the music and the clapping that only she could hear. Then she swept up the broken pottery and sat down primly by the wall.

They had to force her to go down to the village when she fell ill.

During the months when Irene lives at Saint Constantine's she's glad to have company, so I used to go and stay with her for a few days. We didn't talk much.

139

Irene's got used to talking to her sheep, her turkey, Saint Constantine, and her cat.

She also speaks to the tourists who go past along the road below. Saint Constantine's is high up on a hill above the road. Irene comes out under the arches when she feels like it, and when the tourists look right to her, she cries, "Come, water", which means come and have a drink. Most of the time they go up, says Irene, and they even take her picture. She's shown me two or three such pictures that are in colour too.

I like Irene Fotara, 'cause she's sixty and does nice things like a ten-year-old girl. Like that thing with the turkey, for instance. Only a kid would've thought it up. Well, she saw that the turkey had been gathering leaves, hairs, and feathers, then made a nest and sat on it. The poor thing was broody, but there were no turkey eggs around. Irene felt sorry for the bird, so she put some hen's eggs in the nest. The turkey sat on them and wouldn't budge for anything in the world, so to speak. When the eggs were hatched, it was naturally chickens that came out. The turkey fed them, led them to drink, took them for walks, and very proudly at that. On the other hand the hens recognized the chickens. They knew they were their babies and started fighting with the turkey to take the chicks from her. But the turkey had hatched these chicks and knew them as her children. Hens and turkey pecked each other with a vengeance. The turkey was stronger, but the hens were many. I watched them fighting over the chicks and remembered Religious Instruction, the justice of Solomon. If Solomon had been alive and had been there in the big yard at Saint Constantine's watching the fight, what would he have done? The hens had laid the eggs.

But the turkey had hatched them and cared for the chicks. I supposed Solomon would draw a circle with a piece of charcoal. He'd put the chickens inside the circle. On opposite sides would stand the turkey and the hens. But how would they pull the chickens out, since they have no hands?

Irene had a better idea. She created a separate little yard for the turkey and her chicks. And she talked to her and comforted her, "They're yours, my darling. Nobody's gonna take them away from you. And what if they're yellow, they take after their father."

And it's all right to talk to your chickens and your lambs; I can understand that. But she talks to Saint Constantine as well. *That* I've never seen before. And the things she tells him! She talks as if they were close friends or cousins maybe.

We'd finished all our chores and I had to go back down to the village. I'd spent three days up there. Because she was going to have company on the way, Irene decided to come down with me and see how her house was doing.

We locked the cells, put the animals out in the fields with feed and water and then went to lock the chapel.

"Go see if we've locked the kitchen," said Irene. Seeing that was the last thing we'd done, how come she couldn't remember? I realized she wanted to get rid of me for a while, so I hid behind the chapel apse to see what she was up to.

Sure enough, she knelt on the threshold of the chapel, whispered something to herself, then rose to her feet to lock the door and said aloud to the Saint, to be sure he could hear her, "If you want me to come back, fine; otherwise, farewell." Then she locked the chapel door.

My jaw dropped. Fancy her talking to Saint Constantine like that! I pretended I'd just come back from the kitchen. Irene had put on her kerchief looking very pleased with herself.

Along the way I thought over what she'd said, and I realized Saint Constantine surely wouldn't like his little monastery to get dirty or to fall into ruins and him sitting there all by himself. He sees to it that nothing happens to Irene, so she can go up there and keep him company.

I like it so much up there that if I was older I'd go and stay there myself. No one talks, or bothers, or irritates you. If you feel like talking, you talk; if you feel like eating, you eat. And food tastes better there than in the village. It must be because you're sitting under the holm oak looking at the hills and the sea far away in the distance.

But the evening's the best time. There's no electricity at Saint Constantine's. There are some "Lux" and kerosene lamps instead. Irene and I lit a small kerosene lamp, which was really all we needed.

Me, I lay on the low wall under the arches and gazed at the stars. Nowhere else can you see the stars bigger and brighter. But what I'm crazy about are the ships. Four, even five, sail past every night. We know which one is the regular line to Rhodes and which are freighters passing by. They've got all their lights on, and as you can't make out in the dark where the land ends and the sea begins, it looks like the ships are

142

floating in the air. It seems they're sailing over land and hills, that any minute now they'll stop here, in front of Saint Constantine's, and I'll go on board and sail away.

It's drizzling. I don't mind the cold. I'm quite used to being out in the cold; I like it even, it makes me feel peppy. But rain's different. I go in. Mother's still knitting.

"It's raining," I tell her.

She makes a sign meaning "I know." I must get her to talk. I don't like it the way she's so still. I ask her to tell me that story about the rain again, the time when she and her sisters were children and lived at Kalyvato, below Saint Constantine's.

It's only when my mother talks about her childhood that she smiles. And she's always willing to tell me stories from those days, never says no, though she doesn't much like talking otherwise. But now, for the first time, she refuses.

"I can't," she says. "This is no time to reminisce about rain and running barefoot. We've got real worries now, Astradeni. What are we going to do?"

It's *me* she's asking; my mother's asking *me*! But she doesn't wait for an answer.

"It'll be hard for your father to find a job. You saw what's up with Noufri. Maria's got her own troubles. How long will our money last? Here we've got to buy everything, even parsley. How long can we stay in Stavro's flat? And if Father hasn't got a job by the time our money's gone, what then?"

What can I say? I take her hand as I'm standing there beside her. There isn't much carrying on between Mother and me, coddling and such, I mean. She only kisses me at bedtime when she makes the sign of the

143

cross over me. But now it's *me* stroking *her* hair. It's brown streaked with grey, pulled back in a bun. She rests her head on my shoulder. She's crying, I know. Tears come to my eyes too. Poor Mother, what a lot you've been through.

I'm thinking like a grown-up. For the first time I'm thinking about all my mother's been through. So far I've kept worrying about my own troubles only, and here my mother's crying. I wonder how many hairs turn grey every time she cries. She must've got most of her grey hair over our Little Manoli. And if Mother were to die, what would become of me? Now I'm really crying.

She takes me in her arms and wipes the tears from my eyes. It's the first time I look Mother in the face. I mean, for the first time do I look at her *this way*. I *see* her. She's got full lips like her sisters. They're full of tiny lines from being pursed so often. She rarely laughs any more. Her eyes have something of the colour of honey; they're sweet and full of bitterness at the same time.

"Don't leave me, don't ever leave me," I say and squeeze her, as if she's about to get up and go right now.

"I scared you, my darling," she says slowly as if murmuring a lullaby, "I scared you. It's that I haven't got a soul to talk to about how I feel, about what bothers me. On Symi I'd have talked things over with Thareini and got them out of my system. But who can I talk to here? For a moment I took you to be a grown-up, but you're still a fledgling."

We're neither crying nor talking now. The rain's falling in the yard and gives my little fig tree a good rinse. So I swear never to upset my mother again, never make her feel unhappy. I won't tell her that I don't like the school, how the kids are making fun of my name; none

144

of this, whatever happens. I mustn't upset her even more.

I don't know how long we've been sitting like this. Mother's holding me on her knees like a baby. Only when we see the water flooding the room do we jump up. The yard floor is slanted, it seems, and the rain water's pouring into the kitchen. In the corner of the yard there's a broken drainpipe too, and the water's gushing out like a dirty waterfall and running into the kitchen. There's half an inch of water on the kitchen floor. We mop it up and mop it up, but there's always more.

That's the state Father finds us in when he comes home. He's brought us roasted chestnuts and a newspaper, he says. Fancy that! Must be the ways of the capital. We stuff the mop in the crack under the door that lets the water in and sit down so Father can tell us the news. The chestnuts in a paper twist are still hot and smell pleasantly of charcoal fire. There are five chestnuts, one of them rotten.

"Why didn't you get some more?" I ask Father with my mouth full. I feel I ought to give one to Father, one to Mother, and, not counting the rotten one, I'll still have one chestnut left.

"They're five drachmas a piece," says Father. Neither he nor Mother will have their chestnut. He just takes the rotten one, picks the good bits out and feeds Mother with them like feeding a little bird. Blast it, I burst into tears again. What's come over me? Is it the chestnuts, that business before with Mother, the school?

"The child's tired," says Mother. "It's all too new and

145

too much for her, that's why." She wipes my tears and I feel better again.

Father says he met Lefteri at the tailor's. He's on his way to Holland, to Amsterdam, to meet his ship. He told Father he could go along as second mechanic if he wanted to. Father didn't even consider it, of course. Michali "Vriti" told him about an auto workshop where they need a fitter. He's going to look into it tomorrow. That's why he's bought the newspaper, he says, to look at the want ads, so tomorrow he can go to several places to see what's up.

It's the first time Father brings a newspaper home. On Symi he sometimes read a paper at the café. But there they only had the ACROPOLIS, and he didn't much like that paper, as he said. Now he's bought TA NEA, because it's got the most ads.

He turns the pages and finds the place where it says EMPLOYMENT OFFERED. There's a whole page of it. Only near the bottom of the page there's a small column under PLEASURE BOATS. I ask Father to let me read out the notices. I fetch a pen from my school bag, so we can write down all the jobs that seem suitable. I'm going to read out loud and Father will tell me what to make a note of. I'll just read the beginning of each ad, so we don't waste time.

I start: cabinet maker, upholsterer, cook's help, lady wanted by garment industry, programmer, cleaning lady, experienced salesman. (I start getting worried, 'cause I don't see anything that will do for Father.) Young men and women exceptionally gifted to act and dance, theatre career prospects, young people's theatre group, salary, good prospects.

"Look, Father..."

146

"Go on, Astradeni, these things don't interest us."

"All right... personable secretaries, house-help... here's something, employee-collaborator, man 25-35, pleasant personality, to visit customers, School Leaving Certificate."

"Well, my dear, your father's forty-two and hasn't finished school," says Father smiling, embarrassed.

So he's forty-two. I had no idea. I thought he was no more than thirty-five. I go on.

Fashion centre requires experienced saleswoman, furniture Co. requires upholsterers, waiter, schoolbus driver... Here there's something in English, I skip it... Are you enterprising, intelligent, polite? Are you articulate? If so, here's a chance to earn as much as you choose.

"Never mind, I'm neither intelligent, nor a windbag, go on."

"... assistant mechanic for auto workshop..."

"That's it, put that down," says Father.

I put a circle round it and read on.

"Bass... what's a bass, Father?"

"Read on and maybe we'll figure it out."

"Well, it says, 'Bass to sing for recordings and work with pop group'."

"It must be the one who sings the bass part, with a deep voice, that is."

"... fork lift operators free of military obligations required by vehicular refrigerator Co..."

"Put that down too."

"... sheet metal workers, glass fitters, electronics man, polishers, press operators, shirtmakers, buttonhole makers..."

What a lot of different professions! I don't even know what they are. I'd no idea so many specialties existed. We marked four ads out of the whole page.

"The best one," says Father, "is the one asking for a fitter in a Piraeus workshop, five-day week."

That means he'd be working five days a week only. He'd have two days off to stay home and rest. He's going there tomorrow.

But what impressed me most is that women can work and make a lot of money. On Symi women look after the animals, work in the vineyards, or in shops helping their husbands. Only women teachers are paid. They get about fifteen thousand a month, Father says. Here, on this page, I read that a lot of women are needed for work. And they must earn a good deal, because if they make fifteen hundred to two thousand a day working in a bar, imagine what they must be earning in factories and shops where the work is much harder.

I woke up at the crack of dawn this morning before the alarm clock went off. It's a very special day today. It's SATURDAY, and we're going to the Museum. We're going to school without our bags, with just pencil and paper to take notes on what we're told, 'cause we're going to write an essay afterwards. I'm so excited, I can hardly drink my tea. Father's given me ten drachmas to buy a bread-ring or crisps if I want to.

Me and Father leave the house together. He's going to look for work. He's been looking for work all week. He left in the morning sure he'd come back having got a job, but every evening he came home he was depressed and didn't feel like talking. Either they'd already hired somebody else when he got there, or the wages were too low. Either Father wasn't what they were looking for, or they weren't prepared to pay social security contributions. Mother was stewing in her own juice, as they say. She said nothing; she just sat still, knitting. Sometimes she went to Maria's, or Maria came down to us. But Maria's so busy with her daughter's children, there's little she can do for us. Tomorrow, Sunday, she's asked us up for coffee.

I hope she won't tell Father on me. I'll be very cross with her if she does. O.K. she told Mother, and Mother scolded me. But if she tells Father, it'll be a different story. Well, what am I to do, after all, sit in this room all day? And why did it bother the ladies that I was sitting on the steps? I didn't have to go to school till the afternoon. I'd done all my homework too and had gone up and sat at the top of the small staircase.

O.K. I was watching the people going in and out of the house to pass the time. Why did it bother those ladies? It annoyed them, they told Maria, that I was watching them! I know who must've gone to her, that disagreeable one on the third floor, the one who drags her feet when she's walking. And she insists on wearing high heels too, even though she walks so lopsided on them that they're worn on one side till the wood's showing. She seems to have nothing to do all day, so she goes in and out to buy now a packet of rice, then a spool of thread or the FANTASIO magazine. It's just excuses so she can get out of her flat all the time.

Unless it was Mrs. Tassia on the first floor who told on me. It's more likely it was her. She was coming back from somewhere dressed to the nines, with handbag, earrings, perfume, the lot. When she got to the door, she did something odd: instead of opening the door and coming in, she stood beside the bells and pretended to be looking for something. But she was really looking across the street where there was a young man standing on the pavement. He was wearing tennis shoes and a T-shirt with red foreign letters on it. Then Mrs. Tassia came in, and shortly after the young man walked into the building as well.

Or maybe it was Mr. Aleko. He was coming home from somewhere. I don't think he works, he's always at home. To go to his flat he had to go down the stairs where I was sitting. He lives in the basement next door to us. I got up to let him pass. But before I could get out of the way he squeezed into the narrow space of the stairs pressing his body against mine. It was quite revolting, because he was breathing heavily through the nose and stank like mildewy cloth. There's no smell worse than mildewy cloth. Once my grandma Eleni took in the washing in a hurry, because it had started raining. The clothes were still damp, and the rain went on for three days. These clothes got so smelly, she had to wash them again to get rid of the smell. That's how Mr. Aleko smelled.

I don't believe Mr. Sakoulas told Maria. He's very nice. He asked me what my name was and where I came from. Every time I see him he tells me how beautiful Symi speech is. He knows about such things, and his wife's an English teacher. They have two daughters and live on the third floor across from Eleni, Maria's daughter. Some Sunday, says Mr. Sakoulas, I should visit them in their flat, because he wants to write down some Symi words that are ancient. I've agreed to go.

Some big buses are parked outside the school. There are four of them, and we're going to the Museum in them. First we stand in line and go to our classrooms. I'm alone at my desk. George is only sitting next to me when he's on detention.

Guess who's going to read us a report on the Museum today. Petropoulou, of course. She's really teacher's pet. We're not going to see all of the Museum, says Miss, because it's vast.

All four fifth-year classes are going. We get into the Pullman. That's what they call these buses. I sit at the very back. A girl called Katerina's sitting next to me. She asks me what work my daddy does. Hers, she says, is a lawyer. I tell her mine's a seaman. It's true, after all, isn't it? She asks me some other questions like what I think of the "situation", something about peace; I don't understand what she means. The bus is going along a street full of cars and shops. There's nothing they don't sell, they've simply got everything. The bus stops and starts up again suddenly. We're thrown back in our seats. It's fun. Me and Katerina are laughing together. It's the first time I laugh with another kid in Athens and it feels good.

Miss is sitting up front next to the driver. It doesn't take long for us to get to the Museum.

We get off in front of some steps. It's a fantastic, big building. It's got columns and statues all along the front. Many foreign tourists are going up and down the broad stairs.

Presently we walk into a big hall with glass cases. Against the walls are pieces of carved marble and columns. Our class stands at one end of the hall on the left. Petropoulou's holding her sheaf of papers waiting for a sign from Miss to begin. Miss asks us to be quiet, and Petropoulou starts reading.

"The National Archaeological Museum was founded by the Greek State in 1866 and was renovated in 1935. It is an enormous complex of architectural structures comprising over one hundred rooms, wherein..."

What's she saying, bless 'er? I can't understand a word. Good that I'm near a glass case that's got beautiful things in it. They're labelled and I can read what they are.

"... of different epochs, from the prehistoric epoch to the last years of Classical Greek culture. Among the col-

152

lections the Mycenaean Room is unique..."

That's the one we're in. I read it as we were coming into it. It says so on the glass cases too. Who needs Petropoulou to tell us?

"... are also housed the Inscriptions Collection, as well as the Numismatic Collection, both among the best of their kind."

Some report! She went and copied the encyclopaedia; I heard her telling her friend Asbesta.

Miss applauded Petropoulou when she finished, so we had to clap too. Now Miss says we should go round the room very carefully and read the labels, so we know what we're looking at.

Everybody's gathered round the weapons, Agamemnon's daggers. The best cases are surrounded by kids, so you can't see anything. They're very noisy too. But there, on the left, there aren't many people at the cases. They've got women's trinkets in them: necklaces made of coloured stones or tiny shells, paper-thin gold bees. There are dangling earrings, pins and safety pins that held women's dresses. I walk toward the centre of the room where most of the gold things are. There's the mask of Agamemnon made of "gold leaf", as Miss called it, and a pair of scales.

I look at some more, but there's too much noise, and I'm not used to it. There's a small door on the left with a sign that says NEOLITHIC ROOM, and I go in. Here it's quiet. There are only a couple of foreigners and the guard.

"Welcome," he says, "I'm glad you're interested in the neolithic things." I have no idea what the neolithic things are and whether I'm interested in them or not, but I don't tell him in order not to make him feel bad.

"Everybody goes in there to the Mycenean gold; only a few people come here. Yet here's the big step in the history of mankind. I ought to know," says the guard, "I listen to the archaeologists and the guides. Right here at Sesklo and Dimini."

He's got up and is pointing at some pictures on the wall. They show some savages fighting with lances. Then the guard shows me some tools made of stone and animal bones, some necklaces made of shells or pieces of bone, and finally a big jar. The jar's so tall it reaches up to my shoulder. They kept water, or wine, or olive oil in it. There's a dog carved in it. The dog looks very alive to me. I say so to the guard to please him.

"Yes," he says, "I look at him for hours on end while sitting next to him." His chair's right next to the jar in fact. "I've even given him a name. I call him Blackie."

I join my class back in the Mycenaean Room. Then we go out into the hall again and walk around the rest of the Museum. We look at big and small statues, sections of arms and heads cut off. But we also see wonderful bronze statues that are whole, like Zeus or Neptune (they're not sure which of the two he is), some men made of marble, and a bronze boy on a horse.

We get tired of going around. We're quite exhausted. And besides, we're looking at everything all at once. When I wanted to read the label on Aristodicus, who made an impression on me, the rest of the kids had already got to Zeus or Neptune, and Miss called me to follow the others and not stay behind. We should've had a guide too, as the guard said, like the foreigners. Guides know which are the most important things and stop there longer. That way you don't feel lost in this vast museum.

It's still early when we get back to the school. Miss says it's better for us to write our essay now that everything's still fresh in our minds. We're to write as if it were an exam.

Miss writes the topic on the board, "What Impressed Me Most at the Archaeological Museum."

I settle down and write. I write and write, and there's no end of it. Mrs. Antigone, on Symi, always said I wrote "vivid" essays. I wonder whether Miss will like my writing too. It's my first essay in Athens; we'll see. We hand in our papers (we had to write on paper, since we had no exercise books with us) and leave school a little earlier because it's Saturday.

Entering our house I run into Mrs. Sakoulas. She invites me to visit them at five in the afternoon to have cocoa with the girls and talk. I'm delighted, because I like the Sakoulas. He speaks in a slow, calm manner. She's soft-spoken and doesn't put on fine lady's airs. The girls seem nice too.

I'm fidgety and keep looking at the clock. My mother warns me to be on my best behaviour and not to open my mouth and start telling those stories of mine, when there's no stopping me. I keep saying "all right" and "of course" and put on my best dress. Finally at five to five I set off. It's bound to take five minutes to go up all those floors.

I ring the bell. Marianna, the younger daughter answers the door. She's first form and goes to ballet class too, three times a week. What matters is she doesn't boast about it, just mentions it by the way as we're sitting in her room. She's got her own room, together with her sister, that is. Her sister's finishing secondary school. She's not home at the moment. She's taking extra lessons to prepare for her university entrance exams. There's another girl in the room called Jenny, who goes to ballet class with Marianna.

The room is furnished with two identical beds covered with soft pink blankets and a small bookcase with lots of books and some dolls on the shelves.

Mrs. Sakoulas brings us three cups of cocoa with milk. On a dish there are round slices of some sort of white and brown sweet. There are also some other round sweets like chocolate-covered cookies with a cherry on top. My mouth waters, but I don't help myself to any of these right away. I wait, so they don't think I'm starved.

"Go ahead," says Mrs. Sakoulas, "have your milk before it gets cold."

So then I take a couple of slices of that sweet that Marianna's called "cake", cut them into small pieces and dunk them in my cup. The milk almost flows over. It's only milk in a manner of speaking, because really it's cocoa. So I lift my cup to drink a little to make room for soaking some of the cookies in it next. I take up the spoon and fish out the soaked pieces of cake. It's a dream! It tastes divine! I put the soaked sweet slowly and gently into my mouth; I press it with my tongue and swallow the liquid that's now taken on some of the taste of the sweet, and then I swallow the sweet.

But now I see that Marianna's also breaking off small pieces of the cake, but she doesn't dunk them in the cocoa. She puts them in her mouth, and after she's swallowed them, drinks some cocoa. And what's more, without going slurrp like me.

Jenny's staring at me curiously. She hasn't had a bite of anything at all, she's just watching me the way I'm eating. My pleasure's cut short at once. It's as if I have a teacher over my head. It bothers me when someone's watching me like this. So I put down my cup, though there are still three bits of cake in it. I start turning over the pages of a book that Marianna's given me, making as if I'm finished with milk and sweets.

Jenny then starts saying that ballet exercises are becoming harder and harder, but that's the only way for them to face up to the exams. All my enthusiasm is gone. It was stupid of me, I should've waited to see how *they,* those Athenian girls, were going to eat first, and then do as they did. Marianna didn't say anything, of course, but after this they may never invite me again.

Presently Marianna's father comes into the room. He doesn't want to spoil our fun, he says, but would I like to go to his study. Of course I'd like to; I have no business here. I can neither talk about ballet, nor about the movies they're discussing now.

We go to another room. Mrs. Sakoulas is correcting exercise books. I'm shown to a chair and sit down. Mr. Sakoulas opens a drawer and takes out some papers. He tells me he's engaged in a study of the language spoken on various islands, because, he says, the language on Symi is different from the language on Crete or on Naxos.

When I was very young I thought everybody spoke like us on Symi. Later I noticed that the Athenians who came to our island spoke differently. Mr. Sakoulas tells me that Symian Greek has a lot of ancient words in it. He's got them written in a book. In other books he's got the Cretan and Naxian words. He says he wants to find out how many of these words we're still using now, how many of them I know, being the "younger generation". That's what he called me, "the younger generation". It sounds nice, like a game. He'll read out words to me, and I'll tell him whether I know them and what they mean.

So he starts by asking me whether we still say *aera, akatós, adylóna, alós.* Well, of course, what else would we call these things? But I've never heard *alós* and I tell him so. He asks me whether it reminds me of some word to do with *salt*, salty that is. Ah, sure enough, why didn't I think of it to begin with; *spinálo,* of course, that delicious titbit served with wine.

At Pedi and Panormitis, in the summer, we went mad with diving. We competed who would bring up the greatest number of *spínes,* fan mussels, that is. We scraped the meat out of them removing the "little coal" inside that makes the meat taste bitter. But we eat the *glepiós* as well.

"What's a *glepiós*?" asks Mr. Sakoulas.

The *glepiós,* the "lookout".* It's a small shrimp that sits on the edge of the open mussel shell. The shell is half or more than half buried in the sand on the sea bottom. You only see the open top of the shell when you dive. The "lookout" sits on the opening, and as soon as it sees danger from human or crab, it warns the mussel that clams its shell shut. And then, try as you will, you can't pry it open. We salt the meat of the fan mussel and keep it in glass jars to eat in the winter. That's *spinálo.* We make *skaróalo* too, that's salted *skáros* or bream livers. In the old days they used to salt sea snails and other shell fish too.

Mr. Sakoulas seems delighted. He keeps writing down all I'm telling him. Then he asks me about *alopós,* the *náma* of the Holy Communion, and a whole lot more.

He tells me the name of the snake we call *methýra* is ancient too. Who'd have thought it! Its name comes from *myo-théras,* which means "mouse hunter". Then we talk about some other Symian words that come from Ancient Greek. We still use them all. The one I'd never thought could be an ancient word is *tatás,* which is what we call a godfather. Mr. Sakoulas says it comes from *tétta,* a kind of respectful term the ancients used to address older men. If Mr. Sakoulas says so, it must be true.

We then discuss the word *friós* too. I tell him about the *friós* in the "red field" at Saint Constantine's. It's a

---

* *glepiós*, from the verb *vlépo* (variant *glépo*), to see.

very very deep well. The story goes they once dropped a tree trunk in it, and it came out way below in the sea. And before that, they say, they dropped the bow of a shepherd's lute into it, and it came out in Saint Basil's Bay. The *friós* is so deep that it communicates with the sea. I used to put my ear down, next to the mouth of the well and thought I could hear the sound of the waves.

"I could kiss you for all this, Astradeni," says Mr. Sakoulas, "You're a walking history book."

Mrs. Sakoulas, who can hear everything from where she's sitting, stops correcting her exercise books and says, "And to think that these people have been speaking this language for so many centuries, and that most of the words are unaltered."

That's what they said and I was really struck by all this. Fancy that even *vailízo*, to sing a lullaby, is ancient, and that *tatás* is ancient! We've no idea words are so very old, we just talk that way.

When I get back downstairs I start telling them that we speak Ancient Greek on Symi and don't know it. I'm all wound up and talk and talk without noticing how worried Father looks. Today's job possibilities have come to nothing again. He's still without a job. My mother gives me a sign, and, since I'm not hungry anyway, I go straight to bed. I take up the book I borrowed from Marianna to read in bed.

My parents are talking in whispers in the next room. By the time I've got to page eleven of the book I'm sleepy. I shut the book and get up to switch the light off. I lie down on my side, which is how I like sleeping. I look at the wall and imagine seeing all sorts of things on it:

160

little angels, the map of Symi, a lamb. I'm thinking about Don Quixote in the book I've just been reading. Everyone takes him to be mad, but all the poor man wants to do is defend weak people. Is that madness? He also wants to perform great deeds, of course, but I'd better wait and see what happens next in the story.

In church today my mother stood in front of the icon of Saint Phanourios for a long time and her lips were moving all the time. Her imploring eyes were fixed on the Saint.

I'm not staring at the ladies today. I'm praying with all my heart for Father to find a job. I've saved the ten-drachma piece Father gave me yesterday and drop it in the second collection plate.

After church Father and I go to call on Maria Had-zakis. She comes from Symi too. She left the island when she was a young girl and went to Egypt. Many Symians left at that time, when we were under Italian rule. The nearest country they could go to in order to find work was Egypt. After spending many years there, they came to settle in Athens.

Maria Hadzakis is a widow. She's got two grown-up children, a son and a daughter. They live in a house very near the supermarkey. There's a beautiful old house with a marble staircase, balconies and a garden. At the bottom of the garden is Maria's little house. On the corner by the big house is the HEROIC SOULI café. It's got marble-topped tables where all these old men sit drinking coffee or tea. They're also reading newspapers. They read papers that aren't the ACROPOLIS. I've seen them reading the HESTIA, the FREE WORLD and the DAILY.

Next to the café is a green iron gate. It looks like the gate of my old school. It's through this gate you go into

Maria Hadzakis' garden. But the sun can't reach down there. The blocks of flats all around are too tall. Still, she's planted some trees and shrubs: a plum, an acacia, an oleander, and a bitter orange tree. I have all this from Rena, her daughter. Rena's got a thing about cats. She's got Jocasta, Carrot (named because of his colour) and Zouzoulo, the kitten. These are the permanent cats. The kittens they produce are temporary. She either gives them away or takes them to the park. She never drowns them, she says. Maria's house at the bottom of the garden has got two rooms and a kitchen. It's got a toilet too, but no bathroom. High up in one room is a sealed window without shutters. It's the room where Maria's son Yanni sleeps when he's not away at sea. He doesn't like the sea, but there's no other work he can find, Maria tells Father.

We're sitting on the double bed in the main room with a window that can be opened. Maria's thin with grey hair. Mercouri, his brother Themistocles, and Nikitiades are also in the room. They're all old Symians, and they gather at Maria's who's their cousin. Each one in turn buys the coffee for the week, because they drink lots of coffee and smoke. Actually Mercouri smokes secretly. He's had two heart attacks and the doctor has forbidden him to smoke. But he comes to Maria's once in the morning and once in the afternoon to smoke two cigarettes each time. Then he takes a walk "to clean his breath" and buys a chewing gum, so his wife won't notice the cigarette smell and start grumbling.

I'm great friends with Mercouri, actually. He goes to Symi every summer. He goes to the great monastery of Panormitis and to Periviotis, their own little monastery. At Panormitis he kept Father company when we were there with the caique. He's got a nice boat with a motor, and I often went fishing with him. His sons Yanni and Nereus came along too. He's also got a daughter, Lela, but she didn't come fishing with us. Early in the afternoon we used to go to Cape Merthe and drop the lobster pots. We put pieces of bread and salted herring in them for bait. I always liked the way back from the lobster pots. There's a peace at that hour that soothes your heart. The sea is calm, and the sinking sun colours the water red. The boat motor goes doukou-doukou, and the only other sound is the gulls screaming. When I was small I wanted to become a seagull, to fly wherever I pleased, on the rocks, over the sea. But then Mrs. Antigone taught us in Natural History that seagulls are cruel and vindictive birds, and I gave them up. I don't love them any more. But I liked seeing them nesting together with the rock pigeons in those rock hollows just before coming into Panormitis harbour.

In the evenings we sat at Levenderi's café, God rest his soul, next to Panormitis' bell tower and baited the long fishing lines with the many hooks. We baited only when he had small fry or sardines for bait. But such fish rarely strayed into our waters, so we didn't often fish by this method. It was mostly the grown-ups who talked and told stories, till the power was turned off at the power plant.

At the crack of dawn we went and lifted the lobster pots. We usually caught nothing else but those wonderful little red shrimps with the blue intestine. They're tiny shrimps with blue stripes and bulging eyes. I felt sad when we cut them up with a razor to use them as bait. We fished just beyond Sesklia or at Saint Basil's. We caught bogue and horse mackerel when they were in season, as well as large-eyed balas, tunny and red mullet. But it was mostly bogue we caught, and of that I was even given my own share.

Last summer I spent twenty days at Panormitis. I stayed with my cousin Hamiotissa. Her husband George left the sea and became the monastery's baker. He didn't know the trade, but he learned it and likes it a lot. He makes fantastic whole-wheat rusks. The boats stopping there buy them by the sackful. He sprinkles them with black sesame seed that makes them smell nice. He lives at Panormitis through the winter too and bakes for the workmen and the monk. Never a dull moment, he says. Winter, when it's peaceful, is the best time of year. He sits in his little cell, reads a detective story, listens to the thunderstorms raging outside and says, "Thunder all you like, I'm no longer at the helm to be scared. I've dropped anchor right here for good!"

Yes sir, that's George the globe trotter for you, in a cell at the Panormitis monastery and very contented too! When he talked to my father he said he'd never go back to the sea. He may not make so much money, but he's at home with his wife and his son Michali.

"I've made it to home port," he told my father. Mercouri says George has dealt with the matter sensibly, like a philosopher. That's how he put it. Fancy declaring George a philosopher! But if the grown-ups say so, it must be true.

They're very pleased to see my father at Maria's. Mercouri keeps asking about all the folks back home. His brother Themistocles is trying to fix Maria's iron with a file. He's always fixing things. Father says he's a good mechanic. He learned it all in Egypt. He was, they say, a mechanic in the Canal Zone, whatever that is.

I don't know the other one, Nikitiades the old man. I see him for the first time. He comes from Chalki, but he married a Symian woman, Sevastoula, Maria's sister. He too has lived in Egypt. They gather here every day. They don't like going to the cafés. Here they can discuss politics at their leisure, reminisce about the old days on Symi and in Egypt.

They'd all lived in the same neighbourhood on Symi. Then, when they went to Egypt, they lived in the same town. And when they came to Athens at last, they chose to live in the same neighbourhood again.

"That was our salvation," Mercouri once told Father. "Twice we had to move on, but we always stayed together."

I'm looking at Maria's ceiling. It's very high, and it's got damp spots. They've switched on an electric heater that helps a little against the cold. Rena is sitting on the bed wrapped in a blanket. She's got Jocasta, the cat, beside her. She wants to become an actress, she says. Fancy that, an actress, and she isn't even blond!

Mercouri asks me whether I like Athens. What's there to say? I've been here just ten days. It's got everything, I must say, but somehow there's not enough room. Everything's crowded, houses and people. Neither can you find your way around without asking, as you can on Symi.

"There's not enough room," I tell him. There's silence, and they look at me as if I've said the wrong thing. I'm embarrassed. I didn't mean to make them cross. But they aren't cross, as I gather from what Mercouri says.

"Ah, Astradeni, my dear, you've spoken for all of us."

Again nobody speaks for a while. All you can hear is Nikitiades playing tsak-tsak with his worry beads.

"When I left Symi, see, I was just fourteen," says Mercouri. "I arrived at Port Taufiq in Egypt in the night. When God's day dawned I discovered I was in a village. Nothing like the great city I'd been dreaming of. A few little cottages, and everything dry as hell. These sand dunes all around and nothing else. Was that where I was going to live, I asked myself, me who was always on the wing on Symi, who dashed from Yalos to Pedi and from Pedi to Xissos? Me who skipped school with my friends to go fishing at Pitini... 'I wanna go,' I told my aunt. 'Go where, boy! Bein' illegal, seein' you left Symi without no passport, the Italian carabinieri gonna arrest ya the minute you set foot on Yalos.' And she was right. I'd been a stowaway on the ship. A Symian steward had hidden me among the crates. So I couldn't go back. But neither did I want to stay."

Just like me. It was a different sort of Athens I'd imagined. Not that it hasn't got the big shops and the cinemas, no, it's got all that. But I thought it was going to be a place where you'd feel, how shall I say, more carefree. Somehow in Athens you feel depressed. There's no-one to talk to. They're all too busy. They must have a lot of work to do. And yet Father can't find a job. Truth to tell, the supermarkey's got everything the heart desires, but we can't afford it. We're being very thrifty at the moment, of course, as we haven't got enough money. Maybe when Father has a job we'll be

167

able to buy everything we want to. But Maria, who sometimes takes me along when she goes shopping, is always grumbling too. "Everything's getting dearer," she says, "but the pension stays the same." And there aren't any kids for me to play with.

"So a week went past," Mercouri continues, "and I was a-moaning all the time. I was depressed. A cousin of mine, Michali, God rest his soul, was at Combret, that's a Canal station. He sent a message for me to look him up, and I went. There were even fewer houses there and sand as far as the eye could see. But the place was on the Canal, and there were some boats. One night I woke up, 'cause of something dripping on my face. Eh, it must be raining, I thought, but it smelled of fish. The lights were suddenly switched on, and I saw my cousin Michali, God rest his soul," (whenever he said "God rest his soul", the others in the room nodded as if in agreement) "holding two enormous fishes. He'd fished them right there in the Canal. I jumped up, put on my trousers and ran out. There were others fishing too. They gave me a line, and I sat down to fish. That night I caught two huge fishes like Michali's. And the next day, when the boat left for Port Taufiq, I stayed behind. I stayed in Combret to take up fishing. Then they forced me to go to school. In my case, I mean, fishing was the bait to keep me in the foreign land. Later I got used to it."

Again no-one spoke. And I imagined an enormous fishing line with an enormous hook from which Mercouri was dangling. Then I saw myself caught on the fish hook.

"You see..." It's Mercouri's brother Themistocles talking now. I've noticed that when one of them finishes a story, no-one speaks for a while. It seems they're thinking over what the speaker's just said. Then the next man picks up the yarn, always starting with "You see..."

"You see, we baited large hooks with meat and fat to catch crabs. Once at Suez we caught about fifty crabs and wrapped them in canvas soaked in seawater to keep them alive. We intended to stuff them with rice. We took them home and went out to do some shopping. Meanwhile the canvas came undone, and all the crabs escaped. When we came back and found the canvas empty, we were out of our minds. We chased the crabs all over the house, under beds and sofas, behind flower pots, hanging on the curtains, everywhere."

I laughed and laughed. I thought it was so funny, crabs crawling all over the house; so funny!

"Amen that ya 've laughed," says Mercouri switching to Symian dialect. "When ya feel kind'a fenced in, and ya need room kind'a, ya allays be welcome 'ere."

While saying this his small eyes are laughing, as if to say, "I know, my girl, how you must feel in this strange place, 'cause I went to a strange land myself, and, what's more, I was all alone." I knew Mercouri and his brothers had been orphans since childhood and had been brought up by an aunt. He'd told me once when we were fishing, even though us fishermen don't talk on the job; us real fishermen, that is, not those others, the amateuurs.

We had set our nets at daybreak beyond Panormitis and were sitting around. We were having coffee and tea at Levenderi's café, waiting for the time to draw the nets. There were Mercouri, his cousin Dino, and Gabriel, the monk.

Gabriel had become a monk because of a vow. When he was about thirteen, he and his mother were coming home from Rhodes by caique. He'd just had his appendix out. On the way they were bombed by an aeroplane — it was in the war of 1940 — and the caique sank. Gabriel was coming fresh from the operation, as well as being handicapped, because there's something wrong with one of his arms. So he vowed that if he survived, he'd devote his life to serving God at the Panormitis monastery. He fought with the waves for hours and was the only survivor! Since then he's been living at the monastery.

So, as I said, we were sitting at Levenderi's waiting, watching the sun rise, each one of us wrapped in his own thoughts. The world was still asleep. At this point a young Athenian couple appeared. The girl was really a Symian, but he was Athenian. She'd brought him to Symi, so he would get to know the island. Good kids, but inexperienced. They had agreed the evening before to take Levenderi's boat and go fishing. They pulled the rope to bring the boat near the water's edge, got in, went through an elaborate routine till they sat down, and the young hero took up the oars. He certainly hadn't rowed very much in his life; he splashed too much with the oars. We noticed that they hadn't weighed anchor and waited to see what was going to happen. Gabriel was sniggering hee, hee, hee into his beard all the while playing with his worry beads. Mercouri was fidgeting on his chair, saying, "Goodness me, goodness me."

The Athenian rowed and rowed, but the boat wouldn't go beyond the five metres the anchor rope allowed for. He strained at the oars more and more rowing harder, till he saw the stretched rope and understood. He dropped the oars and began weighing anchor, cursing the while, "Damn your mother's island!"

We were laughing to ourselves, so he wouldn't be offended. Only Gabriel couldn't control himself and rushed indoors to roar with laughter.

Father's got up saying it's time for us to go, because Mother'll be expecting us for dinner.

At dinner Father tells us that tomorrow he starts work at an auto workshop in Piraeus. The money isn't very good; they pay less than the basic wage, he says. But it'll have to do, he has no choice. He can't afford to wait for a better job any longer.

But if we economise, even with this money we'll save a hundred thousand in six months maybe, or a year at the utmost. That's how much he needs to buy a small second-hand lathe. Then we go back to Symi, and he'll open a workshop. It'll do good business, because Symi needs a workshop now with all the boats and the tourist business. He'll make screws, bolts, nails and such. So, we'll feel the squeeze for six months or at most a year, but after that we'll have made it!

"Here in Athens," says Father, "you can't get ahead. The overheads are forbidding: rent, electricity, fares, clothes, petrol, service charges, to say nothing of food that's more expensive. Whereas on Symi we've got our own house, our vegetable garden, we may keep a few chickens again (here he gave Mother a sideways glance), and you can go down to Yalos in your old work clothes without worrying about it. Everybody goes around that way. There are no fares, you need no petrol; in short, life's cheaper on the island."

"And better," says Mother, who never says much. I have nothing to say. I don't know any more whether I want to stay in Athens or go back to Symi. Actually I'm rather bored in Athens, but maybe because it's the

172

beginning. After all, life in Athens can't really be like this. Otherwise, why do all these people from the islands and other places flock to Athens to live here? It can't be that they're not living in better places than Stavro's flat, that they're not going out to have fun, dressing well and going to good schools. Otherwise, why would they stay here, why on earth? Maybe now that Father's starting work our life'll change. And maybe he too will change his mind gradually and want to stay.

I really felt very bitter at school today. And I'd been so looking forward to it, because we were getting our essays back. In class Miss returned all the exercise books, except mine.

"I have here," Miss said, "three essays I want the whole class to hear, Hadzipetrou's, Sakinou's, and Petropoulou's."

So first Miss read out Sakinou's essay. That's naughty George, Kyriako's cousin. He'd written a few lines, that's all, and it went like this:

"Today we went to the museum. It had in it those ancient things. I like space ships and rockets. But they haven't got a museum for rockets yet. When they make one, I'll go and spend hours there."

"Well, George," said Miss when she'd finished reading, "when will you stop acting like a smart alec? Is this proper Greek, if you please? Can this be called an essay at all? Ask your mother to come and see me. Now I'm going to read Hadzipetrou's essay to you," she went on.

My hands were trembling with excitement, my fingers were frozen.

"It's the first time I've been to such a big museum. There were beautiful old things in it. There were necklaces and bracelets that ancient ladies used to wear; there were weapons and masks belonging to

174

ancient warriors, as well as statues and enormous vases that are called amphoras.

There are two things in the big Athens Museum that I'll remember all my life long: the boy on horseback, and Aristodicus. I can't say which of the two impressed me most.

The boy on horseback you thought would spur his horse and jump over all fences and ride free beyond all museums all over Greece. He would ride up mountains and down to the plains; he would jump over streams and gallop on without stopping ever.

I think the boy and the horse are the most fenced-in creatures I've ever seen in my life, and Aristodicus is the most wronged.

Nobody looks at him, nobody notices him. Everybody passes him by to stop a few feet further on in front of the statue of Zeus or Neptune. Everyone looks at the huge statue, and no-one, but no-one looks at Aristodicus. I didn't know who he was either. But it struck me that his chest and face were full of marks and scratches. Then I read the label that said he'd been found forty years ago at Mesogia, in Attica, and that the scratches on his chest and face had been made by the farmer's plough.

Here the label is wrong. It should say "the farmers' ploughs", because during the 2500 years that Aristodicus remained buried, thousands of farmers must have ploughed that field. And on the chest of Aristodicus thousands of ears of corn must have grown all those years. And Aristodicus may have lost his beauty through the scratches, but he was good and let the corn grow to feed the people.

That's why I say they're unfair to him. It's unfair

to set him up next to that wonderful Zeus. But we
were unfair too, since we didn't even glance at him.
That's why I dedicate this essay to him."

Did I write all of that? When I start feeling sorry for
something I don't know where to stop. Not that I
wouldn't write these things all over again about
Aristodicus, or the boy. No, I wrote the truth, only, well,
that last bit about dedicating the essay to him, Miss
may find it rather odd. I feel quite anxious now.

"You are a vain creature, Hadzipetrou," Miss said.
"What do you imagine gives you the right to feel sorry
for a work of art? To say nothing of the childish gib-
berish about the other sculpture of the boy on the horse.
I don't know what sort of essays you wrote on your
island, but it's high time you learned how to write a proper essay. I'm going to read to you now an essay that I
consider exemplary. It's Petropoulou's of course.
Sakinou, leave the room and come back with your
mother tomorrow. Only oxen groan, not children from
respectable homes. Get out!"

She cleared her throat, put on that sweet manner she
always seems to save for Petropoulou and began.

"Archaeological treasures from all over Greece are
to be seen in the Athens Archaeological Museum.
They come from Mycenae, the Cyclades, Sparta,
Pylos, Thessaly. Here one may trace the development
of classical art from its initial steps to the creation of
the masterpieces of the Golden Age of Pericles.

One is at a loss what to admire most, the golden
mask of Agamemnon, the *kouroi*, or the statue of
Zeus or Poseidon. For the archaeologists cannot
determine with any certainty whether it is Zeus, in

176

which case he is hurling a thunderbolt, or whether it is Poseidon, in which case he is brandishing his trident. His feet, particularly the toes, are perfectly modelled, and his eyes have even got eyelids. It is a statue cast in bronze and is attributed to the sculptor Calamis. It was found in the sea near the promontory of South Euboea and is regarded as one of the masterpieces of our Archaeological Museum.

Descending the marble staircase of the Museum I felt I was soaring on the wings of elation, proud of being a Greek girl. Like our great poet I wanted to exclaim, 'Oh thou Immortal Genius of those great days of old!'"

"There you are," Miss said. "That's an essay: introduction, development of topic, conclusion; chronological and artistic data. Congratulations, Petropoulou!"

The rest of the day was a washout. Miss asked me a question in Religious Instruction, but my mind was wandering, and I couldn't answer, so she took me to task. During break George and Katerina came up to me. As I have no friends to stroll with, I sit in a corner by myself. I like sitting with my back against the wall. I don't know why, but I feel better sitting this way. The yard is so big and there's such a lot of kids.

George and Katerina told me they'd liked my essay more than Petropoulou's. I shrugged my shoulders instead of reacting as I meant to. I wanted to say thank you, but I shrugged my shoulders instead. So can I blame them if they go away and leave me alone? But they didn't go away. George told Katerina not to be afraid but to talk to me 'cause I'm not a tattletale.

"O.K.," said Katerina at last, "I'm going to tell you something, but you must swear you won't tell on me."

I crossed myself and said, "May I not live another happy day." Katerina looked around to make sure no-one else could hear and said,

"THERE IS NO GOD!"

I jumped up and made to go away. They both took hold of me. I'd taken an oath, George reminded me. What blasphemy! And how does she know there's no God? Mother will never forgive me for listening to such talk. Trembling I asked her how she knew.

She said she'd been thinking about it for a long time. In her father's office she saw poor people who couldn't pay the rent, and they were taken to court to be thrown out of their houses. And they had children too. She saw, said Katerina, that only the cruel and the unjust folks succeeded in this world. Only crooks got ahead, and she was always asking herself whether there was a God who saw all this; and if there was, what was He doing to right the wrong?

So she thought, first she had to find out whether God existed. Most of those she asked told her He did exist. Others said yes but... She had to find out for herself. So last night she decided to do something she'd been thinking of doing for a long time. She was going to blaspheme by showing God five fingers!* — I tried to break away, but the two of them held me tight — She thought, if God existed, He must chop both her hands off for this.

---

* a gesture that casts a curse and is considered highly insulting and blasphemous.

178

"Well?" I asked, and my mouth went all dry.

"Look!" she said, showing me her hands triumphantly. "You see, they're still in place! And if I'm telling you all this, it's because you spoke about unfairness in class, and because Miss was unfair to you too."

Mercy, what on earth can Aristodicus, Miss, or Katerina's father's job have to do with those who are wronged? What's she talking about, she must be crazy. Was I talking about *that* kind of unfairness? What's Aristodicus got to do with God? Besides, if there is no God, I mean *if,* who imprinted the letters in Aunt Annika's loaf? What befell Aunt Annika came from God, said Grandma, because she made bread on Good Friday.

It was around midday on Good Friday, when the church bells were ringing mournfully for the *Epitaphios*.* Aunt Annika had taken the loaves out of the oven and wrapped them in a sheet. She dressed the girls and herself for church. And, as she was picking some greenery to take to the *Epitaphios*, she slipped and fell. Not from a great height; it was a low wall, hardly one metre high. But it was a bad fall, and she was left paralysed. They took her to Rhodes and to Athens. Some bone had been displaced and she needed an operation. She refused to have the operation and stayed that way the rest of her life.

While she was away in Rhodes, her mother, Aunt Sevasti, went to her house to stay with the girls. It was she who saw the bread. They took a loaf from the pile

---

* *Epitaphios*, canopied bier decked with flowers, symbolically containing the body of Christ in Greek churches on Good Friday.

to eat, and Aunt Sevasti saw it had black letters on it. I've seen it with my own eyes, 'cause they've kept that loaf. Aunt Sevasti was a smart woman. She realized those letters were not from a church-bread seal, but as she couldn't read she took the loaf to Father Elias.

Father Elias crossed himself, blessed the loaf and said they were Roman letters. He copied them out carefully on a piece of paper and sent them to Athens to someone he knew who could read Latin.

When the reply came they celebrated a special mass, because it said on the loaf, HONOUR YE MY PASSION; yes, indeed, and in Roman capitals too! They've kept the loaf and show it to anyone who asks to see it.

Fortunately we had singing last period. I didn't sing and no-one noticed. I had a headache. Why, for God's sake did they have to tell me? I've never thought God may not exist. That Katerina, she's got the same name as my mother too, and she's a smart pupil, real smart, not a plodder like that Petropoulou. And she says she's shown God the five fingers and NOTHING happened. God have mercy, I thought, and crossed myself.

When I got home I said I had a headache and went to lie down. It was evening, because we had school in the afternoon that day. I can't get used to those afternoon lessons. Just as lunch warms me up and I feel rather drowsy, I have to go to school. Not to mention that it's already dark when school's out. I kept telling all this to myself in order not to think about that Other Thing about God. It had upset me. They'd told me so unexpectedly. If I'd known they'd tell me such a thing, I'd've sealed my ears. And she said she'd already done it and her hands were still in place. How did she get the idea of trying it this way, showing five fingers, I mean? Why couldn't she think of something else? And if her hands had dropped off, what would she've done then?

Me, if such an idea ever crossed my mind (which is out of the question, but *if,* say), I'd sit on the low wall at home on Symi and say, if God exists, let a cloud appear in the form of an angel. And then, in the blue sky without the tiniest bit of cloud, a cloud would appear white as cotton wool, and it would take the shape of an angel with hands joined in prayer. But what if the cloud didn't appear? That's a silly thought; of course it would appear.

Or I could go to some deserted place without the slightest sound around and say, "Lord, show me that You exist." Then a little bird would come and sit on a stone and sing. And that would've been God's sign that He exists. There's no doubt that the bird would come, and that's that.

God exists! It can't be that He doesn't. For then who would I pray to to save me from the fierce dog, who would I ask to look after our Little Manoli up there? And if, I say *if,* He doesn't exist, what'll become of all of us?

I tell Mother nothing about what happened yesterday. We're having our morning tea together. Actually, I should be telling her now that I need a white blouse for the 25th of March parade. But how can I tell her? We've never felt such a squeeze before. We must save that hundred thousand for that lathe as soon as possible. And the shoes with the strap across the instep for Easter, I must forget them too *for the time being.* Whatever you ask Father and Mother for these days, they say, "Not for the time being. Wait a bit and we'll see."

But the 25th of March parade is tomorrow. How'm I going to go? I thought of falling ill and not going. But Miss told us our "presence is required".

Now the skirt problem can be solved. I can wear my school smock so the lower part serves as a blue skirt. But the blouse? I must definitely find a blouse, 'cause I do want to go to the parade. We're going to lay a wreath at the statue of the hero of the Revolution, Canaris, in the square near our school, Miss told us.

So I tell Mother about the blouse.

"We haven't got one," she says. "Neither are we buying one to be worn just this once. We'll try to borrow one as we did on Symi."

But who from? It's out of the question that Maria will have one. Her daughter Eleni might give us one of young Kyriako's white shirts, but I refuse to wear *his* clothes. He'll broadcast it all over the school and embarrass me. Now Rena, who wants to become an actress, *must* have a white blouse. I tell Mother, and she says I should go ask her.

When I get to Maria Hadzakis' house the oldies are already there. It's almost ten o'clock. Kyriako Senior is there too. Rena's sitting on the bed with Jocasta. What a name for a cat!

"Good to see you, sit down," says Mercouri and goes on talking, "... so, as I was saying, I see this visiting young lady, who was my aunt's godchild too, leaning over and chatting up Yanni Ftakounio who was behind the wall. Hello, here's some goings-on for you, I thought, and she's betrothed to Nikita who's in America!

"I didn't breathe a word to anybody, but in the afternoon, when she'd brewed the coffee, I asked her to turn her cup over and let me read her fortune in the coffee grounds."

"Did you know how?" Nikiforiadis interrupts.

"Aye, and scientifically too. We'd once found a book called COFFEEMANCY that showed all the patterns of houses, trees, horses and such. So I tell the young lady she's not going to marry Nikita, though she's betrothed to him. Instead she's going to marry someone who's right here on Symi. She got awfully scared and asked me not to tell anybody and spread such a rumour. She even gave me a tip for my trouble."

"To keep your mouth shut, not for your trouble," Kyriako remarks.

"And so," Mercouri continues, "two days later a friend of hers looked me up with her coffee cup wrapped

183

in a handkerchief. Many more followed, and I kept receiving money or sweets for my trouble."

"And did you guess right?" Nikitiadis asks again.

"The island was small and gossip was rampant. Who was going to watch his words in the presence of a boy of twelve as I was then? And so an old lady down at Pitini fetched me once. She was a friend of my aunt's. She offered me sweets and said she'd heard a lot about me... and she handed me an upturned coffee cup. She wanted her fortune told too! I knew what was eating her. She needed to marry off her daughter, but the caique that was her dowry, was mortgaged, and the case was in the courts. And the groom was getting impatient. So I told her that what was bothering her would pass and that tangles would become untangled."

"A veritable Pythia!" says Rena, and the rest laugh.

"And so," Mercouri goes on, "this old lady sees my aunt some time after and says, 'Bless your Little Mercouri, he read everything right in my coffee cup'."

My aunt was cross but said nothing to the woman. When she came home she made some coffee and said to me, 'Now sit down and read my fortune in the coffee grounds'."

I sensed something was up, 'cause that devout woman didn't tolerate such nonsense and her face had darkened. So I started telling her I'd no idea about such things. But my aunt was really cross. She took hold of me, twisted my arm behind my back, so I couldn't run away, and took up her cork-soled slipper that really hurt. I got the thrashing of my life!"

The old people chuckle and then fall silent. Mercouri takes out his cigarette holder and starts smoking a cigarette. You can see he's really enjoying it. Even the smoke he exhales he doesn't let go to waste but sticks his nose right in it. He's got a smile on his face like a statue, and his small eyes are looking at something only he can see. Who knows, maybe it's his aunt, maybe the young lady visitor leaning over to talk to someone behind the wall.

Before they get on to a new topic I ask Rena for the white blouse. She gets up, opens a wardrobe in the dark room and produces a white blouse. I guess it'll fit me. I take leave of the oldies and Rena and go.

Besides cats there are some tortoises in the garden. The soil round the trees is pressed flat. It's wet and greenish, as if covered with mildew, as if it's tired of lying there for years without being dug up and having new flowers planted in it. It looks neglected, though it may be the only piece of open ground in the whole neighbourhood. Everything else is covered with concrete, streets or pavements; no earth anywhere, except in flowerpots, of course. But they don't count. They're not a field, real earth.

The sleeves of the blouse are a bit too long and the collar too loose. Mother will stitch up the sleeves under the arms so it doesn't show, but the collar looks terrible and can't be altered... I'll wear my smock collar over it, and that will take care of that.

Anyway, the main thing's I've found a white blouse for the parade.

Today I soaked my hair in water and Mother set it in corkscrew curls. I put on my school smock and over it Rena's blouse. I must be sure to hold my right arm against my side, 'cause there's a black spot on the blouse below the armpit. It couldn't be removed with anything. Mother tried milk and lemon, but nothing doing. Never mind, I'll move my left arm only.

I ran upstairs and stepped into the lift that has a big mirror in it. I can't stop looking at myself. I look quite good. I wetted my finger on my lips and smoothed my eyebrows too! When I stepped out of the lift a lady was coming hurriedly down the stairs in a huff. When she saw me, she said quite out of breath, "What on earth were you doing in there all this time, looking at yourself in the mirror maybe? I had to walk down all the way from the third floor!"

I felt like telling her, "Never mind, it's good for you," but I'm getting in the mood for the parade and don't want to let anything upset me.

I'm walking along on the pavement and looking at myself in the glass of shop windows. I think people are looking at me; I must look good. Approaching the school I hear music, folk dances and such.

Then a whistle goes and we line up. The Head reads out a speech to us. When he's finished the younger ones march into the building. The fifth and sixth years stay behind. The flag and a laurel wreath are brought out. The flag is given to a sixth-year boy who's wearing

186

white gloves. Either side of him stand two other boys. Behind them are three sixth-year girls. The one in the middle is carrying the wreath.

We get into formation, and Miss moves to the back two or three shorties that've gone up front.

"Tall ones up front, short ones at the back! Hadzipetrou, step out of the line!" Miss shouted.

My heart missed a beat. She must've seen my curls, I thought, and wants to place me in the front. She may even ask me to march beside the wreath. But she tells me to wait in the classroom till they come back from the parade, because, she says, I'm not wearing a proper blue skirt.

I stand there to one side. All the kids, even Sakinos, are marching in the parade. I feel like gathering all my strength into a wild run and crashing into Miss.

"Why do you exclude me from the parade," I want to cry. "Don't you see I'm wearing a white blouse?"

But I do nothing. I stand there like an idiot looking at the others marching off, the flag up front, then the wreath, then the rest of the kids. And I so wanted to march in the parade.

Shit teacher, shit school, shit Kypseli, shit people, shit city! I couldn't think of more to swear at... Why, but why, since I'd managed to find a white blouse? Is there no God to see the unfairness of it? I've got to do something, some terrible mischief or a great feat that'll make them all, and especially that teacher, say, "Astradeni Hadzipetrou, we've been unfair to you, please forgive us!"

I wish the school caught on fire, and the doors were

stuck, and the kids were in danger, and then me, I'm running through the flames and smoke from classroom to classroom opening the doors.

Rubbish! As if they couldn't break the windows in case of fire. There's nothing they need me for, nothing. They don't really want me, I'm going away. I'm going to leave school, and Mother and Father, and run away. I'll go somewhere, to a country where the minute they see me they'll say, "Astradeni, we've been expecting you, we're helpless without you." And I'll just nod, as much as to say, "I'm here, I've come to help you."

Balderdash! It's all nonsense, I'm fantasizing again. The fact is they're all marching in the parade, and I'm sitting here alone, the *only* living creature in the whole school yard! I'm not going to wait till they come back. I'm going home. Maybe they'll then worry about me at least, when they don't find me here. Maybe they'll think I've been kidnapped, or killed, or... Rubbish! They'll think nothing of the sort. They won't even remember I was to wait for them here.

I take off the blouse. I almost tear off the collar. I undo the pleats we've put in the sleeves and throw the blouse on the bed. Then I take the broom to sweep Saint Constantine's yard, our little back yard, that is. I sweep it all the time, and all the time it's filthy with rubbish dropped from above. They shake their carpets, their bedding, they drop their cigarette ends and make my little yard a mess. My little fig is budding. It can't produce any figs, of course, but it's bound to have leaves. So my yard'll have its holm oak as well.

Michali, Irene's son, once brought her two tunny fish. So Irene and me lit a fire to grill them.

"I'll show you a trick of my mother's," said Irene, "that makes fish taste twice as good."

She grilled the fish as usual, but without salting them. Instead, she mixed water and salt in one bowl, and olive oil and lemon in another. When the fish were done, she dipped them in the salt water first, and then laid them in the oil and lemon sauce. And I must say, that was the most delicious tunny I've ever eaten.

And what if it was. I'm too upset today to bother remembering grilled tunny and salt water. I don't give a damn! I want to go back to Symi, to my old school, my classmates, my neighbours, my friends, back to my cousins, my teacher, Matitsa, our grocer lady, to our postman, our home and my own little corner in it.

But it's out of the question right now. I've got to wait till we've saved the money we need.

And now, what shall I do with myself? How'm I going to pass the time? It's still morning, and nothing to do this afternoon either, nor tomorrow, 'cause it's the National Holiday. When there's school and homework, I've got something to do at least. But what shall I do today?

I think I'll just go to Davakis' to look around. He's got a haberdashery on the corner. He lets me browse in the shop. He doesn't throw me out like Mr. Haralambos at the supermarkey.

I liked going to the supermarkey. I browsed among the shelves of boxes of sweets, exercise books, coloured pencils and scents for ladies. But I had to buy something too. So I did the same as the old lady on the first floor: one item each time. One day it was salt, the next a packet of spaghetti, or some olives, or paper napkins. So me too, I'm picking up these Athenian tricks.

Yet the last time I was there, Mr. Haralambos insulted me. He embarrassed me in front of all those people. I'd taken a basket (I've learned the system by now) and put a bag of sugar in it. I didn't need anything else, but I pretended I was looking for "something" and couldn't find it.

At this point Mr. Haralambos came up to me, and, after going through my pockets, asked me what I was looking for. I was in a fix. If I'd said I didn't need anything else, he'd have scolded me. So I told him I wanted crisps. He put a packet in my basket and led me to the cashier. But I only had enough money for the sugar. They put the crisps back on the shelf and told me not to come to the shop again, and that I was lucky Mr. Haralambos hadn't found any stolen goods in my pockets, for then he'd 've called the police.

I was mighty scared that time. I didn't sleep at all well that night. I'm afraid of the police; not the Symi gendarmerie, for there we know the gendarme and the officer and everybody. And they know us too.

But here in Athens they've got the police, a lot of police, some for the traffic and some for the people. George Sakinos explained it all to me once. So the policeman doesn't know you, and neither do you know him. It's a puzzlement. He may take me to prison, or make Father lose his job. We can't afford to have any such thing happening to us, so I never went back to the supermarkey.

"It's called supermarke*t*, with a 't' at the end." It was young Kyriako who told me and made me repeat it until I'd learned it. He went on making me repeat it, even after I'd learned it, that is, and his mother finally scolded him. It was when I was in their flat once. He'd come and asked me to go play with him upstairs, and I went.

He's got a room of his own too, together with his small brother Philip. Philip's not so small really, he walks and can speak already. Kyriako pulled a drawer open and produced hundreds of little cars, people, shovels, boats, pirates, teeny-weeny swords, cups, a carriage, a whole lot of little houses. He said these things are called Dinky-Toys and he wouldn't let me touch them. Then he produced what he called an auto route. It was something like a road with curves and little cars rolling on it. He didn't let me touch that one either, because it's a boys' game, he said. Then he brought out a train, a real little train. You plugged it in and it rolled on its rails. You pressed a button and it stopped; you pressed another button and it started rolling again. It rolled past little houses, between mountains, through a forest. I liked the little train a lot. It felt as if I were in it travelling.

I've never been on a train. I told Kyriako and he burst out laughing. He rushed to tell his mother, so odd did it sound to him. I hadn't been on a bus either. And I didn't like being in his father's car that time. I prefer walking. I asked him to let me press the button once to start the train, but he wouldn't allow it. He said we should go watch television. Fancy him having so many beautiful toys and wanting to watch TV! The boy must be crazy. No, he said it 'cause he didn't want me to play with his toys.

We sat down to watch TV. His mother gave us biscuits. Philip bit into a biscuit and then put it down. Pretty soon most of the biscuits were bitten into this way and left lying around. There was a film with rockets and space ships on television. Kyriako was watching with his mouth hanging open and a half-eaten biscuit in his hand. He forgot he was eating. In the film a girl with a bird's beak and a cape was trying to pierce some sort of mechanical gadget with a kind of skewer. I don't like such shows; they're too scary and give me nightmares afterwards. I'd rather have been in Kyriako's room. If they'd been showing a Greek picture or song numbers, I'd 've stayed, but that stuff I could do without.

I got up and quietly left the room. I stopped briefly at the door before going out. Kyriako was too absorbed in the show to notice anything, and Philip was squashing another biscuit on the table. I went back into his room.

I decided to play with the Dinky-Toys for a while and then with the train. But if Kyriako came in before I got to the train? I thought I'd better start with the train.

Well, I was going to be the driver, the first woman train driver. I'd get into the papers and be shown on television. "Today," they'd announce, "the train rolled with the first woman engine driver at the controls." And they'd show me in uniform and hat waving to the crowd. I'd start the engine and the train would roll. Here I pressed the start button. Now I had to show what I was worth, 'cause the train was going through a forest, and then it was going to go uphill. In the mountains I fancied there'd be an attack by robbers, but I'd be very brave, and, increasing speed (here I pressed the other button that made the train go faster) I'd get away from them. One of them, their chief, say, would be galloping beside the train. I'd be able to see him through the window but he'd soon give up the chase.

Kyriako came running in, pressed the stop button and pushed me aside.

"It's mine!" he said, as if I'd claimed it was mine. He was acting like a child, and I told him so too. Why had he invited me then, to watch *him* play? I said I didn't give a damn, I was going home.

I never went back to Kyriako's house. Neither did he ask me again. That's why I say I'll go to Davakis' now. It's quite a haberdasher's; it's got everything, sweets, cigarettes, biscuits, nail clippers. Davakis refills cigarette lighters too. I've seen him going fsss! when refilling them. He sells night-dresses, children's underwear, embroideries, lotions — everything. I go in and stand on the left where there's a little aisle with a glass case full of rings, brooches, necklaces and artificial flowers. I'm very fond of such things. There's a brooch that I like an awful lot. It's a girl with ribbons in her hair carrying a basket of fruit. Every time I go in, I look to see whether it's still there.

Today it's hard to squeeze into the aisle. Anna, Davakis' daughter, is rearranging the shop window on that side. She's dusting. Easter's coming up, you see, and she's got to decorate the window accordingly. I offer to hand her drawing pins and whatever else she needs. It's a good deal, and I'll spend the time pleasantly.

At one end of the display window we put the bibs, rattles and other baby stuff. I hand Anna the Easter candles carefully, and she hangs them on a ribbon. In no time she's hung twenty different sorts of candles in the window. Now, here in Athens, Easter candles look different. They're round or square and come in all kinds of colours, red, green, striped, spotted, or covered with things like little bumps even. On Symi we just have white candles for the Resurrection Service and dark yellow ones for the *Epitaphios* on Good Friday. On the girls' white candles we tie a pink bow and on the boys' a pale blue one. Well, Athens people must celebrate a fancy Easter with all those beautiful candles.

Now I hand Anna Easter eggs covered with red silk to decorate the window with. She puts little yellow chicks among them too. Two kids have stopped outside and are looking into the shop window. They must find it funny, seeing that very tall Anna among the candles and the chicks. So I push my head through the curtain at the back of the window and stick my tongue out at them. The kids laugh and so do I. But I'm careless as I pull my

194

head back and knock down one of the tapers that cracks across the middle. What happens now? Are they going to ask me to pay for it? But I haven't got any money.

Anna looks very cross and says, "I can do without your kind of help. Go before you bring the whole lot down."

Now I'm standing outside by the door looking at the magazines: *Mickey Mouse*, *Popeye*, *Manina*, *Boy*, *Black*, *The Helmet*, *Tarzan*. Do kids buy all this stuff, and where do they get the money? On Symi we've got neither the money nor the magazines. Well, from time to time *Mickey Mouse* or *Popeye* appeared, but it was Sotiria who bought them, and gradually all of us got to read them till they were in tatters in the end.

Next to me a lady's on the phone. There's a big red public telephone Davakis has got out here. I can't hear what she's saying, 'cause she's speaking in a low voice, confidentially. I'm beginning to feel bored, so I make my way home.

There's a lady there mopping the stairs. I'll just stay and watch her, unless she asks me to go away. She's shaking the door mat violently on the pavement and then stamps it down hard. Where does she find so much strength, she's such a tiny woman. She leaves the pail, mop and AJAX on the steps and we get into a conversation, but it's hard going. I don't understand what she's saying, neither does she understand me. I tell her I come from Symi. She says she comes from Ashketh.

"No, Tashkent."

I've never heard of the place; is it in the Peloponnese or Macedonia maybe?

"No, it's in Russia." So she's a Russian, that's why I can't understand her.

"No, no, I come from Samarina in Epirus."

While speaking she shifts the flowerpots about to sweep under them. She's quite skinny with her hair in a knot at the back like Mother. Well, I'm thinking, she's a stranger in Athens like us, *and* she's wearing her hair in a knot like Mother, so maybe we can become friends.

Her name's Athena and she's got two small children. It looks as though she's got no husband. She must be a widow if she's doing this kind of work. Her husband, she says, is a construction worker (so she *has* got a husband after all), but he's got a bad back and isn't working right now. Poor thing, she's worse off than us. With us, at least, Father's fit and he's got a job. Only one out of every five sentences she speaks makes sense to me. It's the same with her. Anyway, we understand each other in the end.

I ask her to come downstairs and meet Mother. Next time she comes to do the stairs, she says, because she's got her little boy with a temperature right now and must rush home.

So now I'm no longer worried about the cracked candles. I've met Athena and we talked, and she may be calling on us. I've never asked anyone to visit in the flat before. I'm ashamed of it, it's not even ours; it's Stavro's.

Stavro came by the other day. He looked handsome in his sailor's uniform. On his cap it said PALASKAS. He stayed just long enough to have a cup of coffee and said we shouldn't bother about him at all. Even when he's off duty — that's what he called it, *off duty* — he can stay with his aunt. Father told him we'll be paying rent for as long as we stay in the flat. Well sure, we can't overdo it, taking advantage of his hospitality now that Father's got work.

196

Tomorrow's Lazarus Saturday, last day of school. I don't really feel one way or another about school closing. I've got no friends, anyway, to walk up and down in the school yard with. Only George and Katerina speak to me now and then. But I don't really want to have too much to do with Katerina somehow, ever since all *that* about God and the unfairness business. Besides we'll have a lot to do at home during Holy Week and I won't get bored. We'll have to bake biscuits, Easter bread, dye eggs, not to mention all the hours we'll be spending in church. On Symi, Easter's our biggest feast. There's a special schedule for every day of Holy Week. You know what you've got to do on the Monday, or on Maundy Thursday, or on the Saturday. I like that very much, I don't know why.

I've already spoken to Mother. Tomorrow I'm going to go around singing for the *lazarakia*. I'm going alone, since there are no other kids to go with. I've found a small basket too, and I'm going round to the flats in our block only.

On Symi we go around in groups. One boy we dress up in a sheet. He stands for Lazarus come back to life. We go to all the houses and sing the Lazarus song. The housewives give us eggs to put in our baskets. They also give us *lazarakia,* little buns, that is, made with walnuts, almonds, sesame seed and spices. And as we've been fasting all during Lent, they seem delicious to us. So today Mother and I baked *lazarakia* for the children who'll come to sing to us tomorrow.

The other day my parents and me decided not to consider ourselves in mourning this year. Except we won't have red eggs; we'll dye them brown with onion skins instead. That — to dye eggs red, I mean — Mother would simply not have. For the rest she gave in for my sake. She senses I feel like a bird stuck on a limed twig or imprisoned in a cage, without friends – who, *me,* who was so popular on Symi, 'cause I was neither a cheat at games nor a tattletale. Besides, I made up games out of my own head that the kids liked. And Mother understands, too, that I'm having a tough time at school. I work three times as hard as on Symi not to give Miss an excuse to pick on me. And I keep trying not to speak the Symian way. And when she addresses me as Urania, I say "Yes, Miss". What can I do, it can't be helped.

Mother and me are taking the baking dish with the *lazarakia* to the bakery. I'm mentioning this 'cause Mother doesn't leave the flat very often. Not that she likes staying home, but what's there for her to do outdoors? Maybe they've even made fun of her out there at some time or other. She doesn't go to Maria Hadzakis', she says, because only men visit there. Father laughed at this, saying she should really go, they're friends, our people, but she won't budge. She talks to Athena sometimes. Mother goes upstairs and keeps her company while she's mopping the stairs. They talk. And twice, besides, my mother cleaned the windows for her. But afterwards Athena got scolded, so now Mother just keeps her company.

That Athena's been all over the world. There was war, she says, in her village, and because the people were afraid they fled into the mountains. They only took a

198

loaf of bread with them. They'd even left the keys in their doors. But the village was taken by the "others". And the people, and Maria with them, were afraid of those "others" and fled across the border into Albania. Then they were taken by ship to Rumania, and from there they were sent to Tashkent in Russia. There she stayed for almost twenty years. Athena left Greece when she was twelve and returned when she was forty, married with two children. But she doesn't want to go back to her village, she prefers it here in Athens.

From Athena's story I remember these words especially: "Even our house keys, we left them in the doors."

Today I dress up, take my little basket over my arm, and leave the flat. I first call on the old woman next door. She never goes out. Some lady comes two or three times a month and brings her food packages. I ring the bell and the old woman comes to the door. In the back I can see the fat lady in the men's pyjamas again. I sing the Lazarus song.

> Tell us, Lazarus, what you've seen
> Down in Hades where you've been.
> I've seen horrors, I've seen frights,
> Suffering and painful sights.

"Perish the thought!" exclaimed the old woman. "Why, the idea, you damn croaker, you!" she screamed and slammed the door in my face.

My mother, who'd heard it all, opened the door and said, "Never mind, you just get on with it. She's an odd bird, don't bother."

At Mr. Aleko's no-one answered the door. I went up to the ground floor, to the flat where the baby cries. They dropped five drachmas in my basket! What an idea! It's eggs they're supposed to give, white uncooked eggs. We'll dye them along with ours on Maundy Thursday for good luck. Well, maybe the lady had no eggs so she gave me money. Never mind, I suppose it'll have to do. I went to all the flats in the block. Some said, "Go away." Others gave me money. Only Maria gave me eggs.

Maria, bless her, when she saw me singing with the basket over my arm, she burst into tears. She hadn't heard the Lazarus song for forty years, she said. But we sing it every year on Symi without fail. She gave me five eggs, kissed me and made me sing the Lazarus song again for Kyriako Senior to hear too. Here in Athens, she said, they haven't got this custom of singing the Lazarus song.

"And what do they do instead?" I asked.

"Nothing," she said, "nothing."

I found that very odd but said no more. Later I took one of the *lazarakia* to her, and she was very pleased. We gave some to Mr. Sakoulas and to Eleni, Maria's daughter, too.

On Symi we normally bake our Easter biscuits in the week before Palm Sunday. But here, since we're having only a few for good luck and for keeping the custom, we're baking them on the Monday of Holy Week.

More than ever Symi fills my thoughts now that Easter's coming. I don't know why, but it was different back home. It was like grandparents who you know well and who never change. In the morning they drink their mountain tea. In the afternoon, always at the same time, they eat their yoghurt, and they always go to bed at the same hour. It's the same with Easter. I mean you knew that now you'd be taking the *kollyva** to church. After the priest had read out the names of the dead over it, you'd stand on the low wall outside and share it out to the people. And they'd say "God rest his soul," and "May you live long to preserve his memory," and they'd all know they meant our Little Manoli, and Grandma Eleni, and Grandpa Sotiri, and all the rest of our dead. Because everybody had known them. Some, that were as old as Grandpa, had been his friends. Others were schoolmates of our Little Manoli.

On all four All Souls' Saturdays that we took *kollyva* to church here in Athens, they told us to empty it into huge baskets. From those baskets the verger dished it out to the people who said, "God rest his soul," but

* *kollyva*, boiled wheat mixed with sugar and spices, taken to the church at memorial services for the dead.

whose soul? They just said it without knowing. Even the dead are all dumped topsy-turvy together here. Nobody said "God rest your Little Manolis' soul." That hurt me a lot, 'cause we'd made our *kollyva* for Little Manoli most of all. That's what I think anyway.

And then you go to such trouble to make the *kollyva* look good with all the almonds, the pomegranate seeds, the raisins, the parsley. On the sugar icing you take the trouble to make crosses and patterns, and all in order to go plop! and dump the whole thing into the basket. May God forgive me for having such thoughts today, as it's a holy day.

But something keeps worrying me. Tomorrow's Palm Sunday, and where are we to find myrtle? We must make up our bunch of myrtle today. We must tie together a couple of myrtle twigs, some thyme, and some rosemary. Then, in church, they'll give us the cross made of woven palm leaves, and an olive twig. I ask Mother. Maria's told her they sell the bunches ready made at the church.

"And is that proper?" I ask Mother.

"If it's proper for the Athenians, it's proper for the Symians."

Well, she sounds cross; as if she doesn't really like the idea of them *selling* the myrtle bunches, but never mind.

Now what they did actually sell at church were these little bunches of palm leaves with some flowers among them.

"It's myrtle I want," Mother kept saying, but nobody had any idea what she was asking for.

"Myrtle, dear, don't you see. What am I to burn in the censer, dried flowers?"

Because the most sacred incense is with myrtle. It removes the influence of the evil eye. Whenever someone's cast the evil-eye upon me, Mother burns myrtle in the censer. I wave the smoke three times toward me with my right hand, and the evil-eye spell is driven out.

We bought those things they were selling after all. There was nothing else to do.

Church is out at eleven. Our meal is scheduled for one o'clock. We're having fish cooked in the oven. I ask Mother to take me to the swings. I see them on the way to school, and I always beg her to take me, but she won't. Yet today I manage to talk her into it. Father's gone to Maria Hadzakis' to join the oldies.

It's a beautiful sunny day and everybody's out of doors. Most people are leaving town by car. Everybody and his brother's at the swings. The kids are queueing up waiting their turn. Mother doesn't want to stay, but I talk her into it at last. We sit on a bench. A woman's sitting next to us. She looks like Mother. She's dressed the same way, in black, so she must be in mourning too, and her hair's pulled back into a bun.

I waited quite a while till my turn came. I started swinging. The tall houses opposite kept moving toward me, and then again I swung away from them. I went higher than everybody else. I leaned my head back and could see the eucalyptus upside down. It was wonderful! But then a lady said:

"That's enough now, get off so some child gets to swing too. You're a big girl, after all."

I felt very embarrassed. Fancy me a big girl! I looked

around to see whether anyone had heard, but fortunately people had been looking elsewhere.

I went back to Mother. She was talking to the woman next to her. Well, it was the woman talking to my mother really. She was a stranger in Athens too. She came from Aetoliko, a place near Agrinio. I said "Aha," as if I knew the place. They'd owned a kiosk there, her husband, that is. But they couldn't make ends meet, so they sold it and came to Athens. Her husband had bought himself into a *concierge's* job. I asked her where, and she said it was a block of flats in Tenedos Street. Her son works for HEBE, the orange juice firm, and her daughter works in a carton factory. They're saving money to buy a two-room flat for the daughter's dowry.

"Are you here with a grandchild of yours?" I asked her. No, she said, but she feels the walls of the basement flat closing in on her, and she comes here to the eucalyptus trees, among the children, for a breath of fresh air. So there are others who feel the walls closing in on them; I'm not the only one. My mother shook her head as if to say, "Everyone's got his own troubles, but we're really all alike." That's what I took her to mean anyway.

"We," I said to the woman, "are going back to Symi, as soon as we have the money for the lathe."

She said she hoped so, because they keep saving and saving, but prices for two-room flats keep going up and up. So the money's never enough.

That hadn't occurred to me. Can it be that we too will be saving and saving, and the price of the lathe will keep going up and up?

I asked Father at lunchtime. He said maybe the lathe would become more expensive, but we'd be able to afford it just the same. I asked him how much we'd saved this month, since he'd started working. Very little, he said, but it was the beginning and we needed lots of things. Starting next month we'll tighten our belts for good and save more.

In the afternoon Mother and I dressed for church. She let me carry the Prayer Book. How well I know this Prayer Book. I've been carrying it for years during Holy Week. I know just where the candle dripped on it. Let me see, yes, sure, it's Maundy Thursday, page 455 where it says, "thou hadst no dominion over me..." and on the edge, in the white margin, a bulging drop of wax. It was three years ago, when I was holding my candle carelessly and it dripped on the Prayer Book. I could've scraped it off, but I like it this way. I want to look at it always in the same place to give me a feeling that everything's the same, nothing's changed.

I like to follow all that the cantors and the priest say in the Prayer Book, even though they confuse me sometimes. But I know all the canticles by heart. Today they'll read, "Behold, the Bridegroom cometh in the middle of the night; blessed is he whom He shall find watchful, unworthy he whom He shall find slothful."

On Symi the whole church is covered in black on this day, the lecterns, the candlesticks, the warden's pew, the icons, the candelabra, everything. Even across the central arch of the altar screen a black curtain's draped. And when they've chanted, "Behold the Bridegroom cometh..." they place the icon in the middle of the church where we go and worship it.

When we got to church the service had begun. They

were chanting, "Lord save Thy people." The church was full. We squeezed into a corner, but I couldn't see anything; I could only hear. I opened the Prayer Book and followed the text. At one point when I heard the cantors humming, mm, I remembered the boy I used to like. Will he be thinking of me as well, I wonder? How nice it would be if, just at this moment, when I'm thinking of him, he thought of me too.

First we kneaded the dough for the "sugar biscuits" 'cause they take a long time to rise. We're baking two sorts of biscuits, the "sugar" and the "butter" ones. And on the Wednesday of Holy Week we bake the "tarts". We're only making a few of each for good luck this year, not like the troughs full of dough we kneaded on Symi before we lost our Little Manoli.

After the "sugar biscuits" have risen and we've baked them, I'll dip them in rose water and Mother'll sprinkle them with powdered sugar. This has got to be done three times. It's a bother, but then they taste better than *kourabiédes,* our sugared walnut biscuits.

The "butter biscuits" are made with butter and flour only. They're hard work, 'cause they need a lot of kneading. Mother'll also make me an *avdokoula.* I'll hang it on the wall above my bed and leave it there until next year. Actually it's my godfather who should give me an *avdokoula* with a red egg in it, but he's on Symi. So my mother made her favourite shape in dough, a fish holding a red egg in its mouth. My godfather used to bring me a different *avdokoula.* It was in the shape of a girl with a red egg under each arm, and she had cloves for eyes.

We brushed the biscuits with egg yolk and took them to the bakery. We also made a *tahini** soup for lunch. We were busy with the biscuits till it was time to go to

---

* *tahini*, sesame seed oil.

church. The "sugar biscuits" turned out good. Not that we tasted them, seeing we're fasting, but they looked good, I mean.

But the "butter biscuits", forget it! My mother was fit to burst. She said it was the fault of the butter and the flour. All these years my mother's never had a disaster with biscuits... Such a thing this time! You took up the rolled-out dough to cut it into strips and it cracked. "Low-grade flour, low-grade butter," grumbled my mother sighing and being very cross. "... and going to all that trouble and expense."

Today's a very important day, Maundy Thursday. Tomorrow's very important too, of course, and so on till Sunday. In the morning, after church, we decided to dye the eggs. Actually, on Symi that is, we hard-boil them with almond leaves and then dip them into the red dye. But where shall we find almond leaves here? The almond leaves give the eggs a yellow hue, which then gives their red colour a special brightness. But, as I've said, this year we're having brown eggs dyed with onion skins. We've skinned about two pounds of onions. We only use the dry outer skins. We soak them in water in a big pot and then let them slowly come to the boil. Meanwhile I, who like this job above all, carefully spread on each egg celery, parsley and dill leaves, as well as small leaves from Mary's flower. I tie the leaves tight on the egg with thread, so they won't move. When the eggs are boiled and dyed, they'll be brown and the leaf shapes will come out yellow or greenish depending. Then we go over them with an oiled cloth to give them an extra shine.

I saw the eggs Maria dyed. They were all sorts of colours. There were red ones, but blue and green ones also. How peculiar! Since Easter eggs are to remind us of Christ's blood, how come they can be blue and green? To say nothing of what Eleni did with Easter eggs. She had speckled eggs, striped ones, pink ones, a real tutti frutti! They must be out of their minds in Athens.

We need silk thread for this evening. I gave Mother some from my embroidery box. She picked out three pieces, white for me, blue for Father, yellow for herself. After every Gospel that's read this evening, Mother will tie a knot in each piece of thread. So there'll be twelve knots after the Twelve Gospels that are read on Maundy Thursday. Then she'll wrap each knotted thread in a small piece of cloth and sew a triangular talisman for each of us to wear till next year when she makes a new set.

The church was full again. We wanted to go upstairs to the women's section, but they wouldn't let us, 'cause it was too crowded, they said. So we stayed below. Just before the Sixth Gospel I knew the priest would come out of the Holy of Holies carrying the Crucifix to say, "Today is hung upon the Cross..." I stood on tiptoe but couldn't see anything except a bit of the top of the Cross. I didn't really enjoy the service.

On Symi it was different. The church looked beautiful, and after church there were nice things to do. We took along incense, coals, censers, candles, and matches. After church we went up into the hills to burn incense before the icons in the little monasteries. We went to Saint Constantine and Saint Nicholas. Other people went to the other places. No little monastery or chapel was left without incense. We burned the incense and said, "Today the sky is black, today the day is black, to-day was crucified the Lord of all creation." We chanted this verse on the way there and back. Everyone did. You saw the lights in two's and three's in the darkness of the hillsides. You could see no people, but you heard the sad chanting, and then something came over me and I wanted to cry. I don't know, but I'd the feeling we all of us were meeting somehow with our little lights and sad verse, meeting somewhere else beyond Symi.

We went back home. On the way Mother kept sighing. Who knows what was on her mind. She had a worried expression, so I didn't talk to her. Father had gone to bed already. He gets up at five in the morning, as he needs an hour to get to Piraeus. But tomorrow's Good Friday, he doesn't have to get up so early. He starts work after twelve.

I know Mother'll be drinking a mixture of vinegar and water all day tomorrow. She won't put anything else in her mouth. Only after the *Epitaphios* service will she have a bite of something to eat.

It was suggested we should go to the Home for the Incurables for the *Epitaphios* service. There's a chapel next to that big hospital. The Home is full of patients who can never be cured, Father's told me. The *Epitaphios* had been decorated by the nurses and was surrounded by men and women in wheelchairs because they can't walk. It made me sad to look at them. From cigarette boxes Father has cut out round cardboard discs with a hole in the middle for our tapers, so the hot wax won't drip on our fingers. We bought three brown tapers at Davakis' shop for tonight.

They had music too at the Home chapel. Sailors with trumpets, clarinets, and drums were marching slowly at the head of the *Epitaphios* procession playing sad music. They were followed by the nurses, then came the *Epitaphios,* the priests, and the cantors. We followed the procession around the building.

On the way home Father remembered how in the old days they used to give out tiny pieces of the four tapers of the *Epitaphios.* These pieces of candle were given to the owners of caiques, and they kept them in the holy icon corner of the caique. They said that in a big storm, if you lit that piece of taper and threw it into the sea, it calmed the waves.

We'll celebrate the Resurrection and Easter Sunday all by ourselves. Maria and her daughter Eleni are going to Rafina where Maria's other daughter has a house. The Sakoulas family are going to Yannina. Mr. Aleko and his wife are going to Kalamata. Yesterday they all started going away. Those people on the ground floor, where the baby cries, are going to Levadia, those living opposite to Astros. Mrs. Tassia says she's going to her daughter in Domokos. The lady who drags her feet says Easter must be spent in one's village with one's relatives.

I find this quite surprising. I mean, in our block of flats, if you leave out the two ladies on the fifth floor, that other lady on the ground floor, us, and the old woman next door, everybody else is going home to their village. Us too, if it weren't so expensive and our island were nearer, we'd be going to Symi, which leaves just the old woman who's got nowhere to go. In other words, like us, they've all come to Athens from somewhere else. How many years ago, I wonder, and did they like Athens from the start?

I wasn't wrong in my hunch that these Athenians have no soul. I kind of sensed it all during Holy Week without being able to put my finger on it. I said to myself it must be the sadness they feel that makes them this way. But on the night of the Resurrection it all became crystal clear.

It was chilly for the end of April, and as it was night-time, we put on our heavy jackets. Our soup was ready; we'd just have to add the egg-and-lemon sauce to it when we came back. This year we weren't having the traditional *mayeritsa* soup made with the offal of the Easter lamb.

"That's not for us this year," Mother had said. "Don't you see how lamb prices have rocketed? Let's buy a chicken. After the Resurrection we'll have the broth, and on Easter Sunday we'll have roasted chicken with potatoes."

Well, Mother's a remarkable housewife. She chopped the chicken livers fine, added dill and spring onions, and made a real *mayeritsa,* as far as smell went, that is. As for the taste, that remained to be seen.

So we set out with our white candles complete with cardboard discs. I was holding a plain candle for grown-ups too. Since my godfather's on Symi, he couldn't provide a candle for me, could he? We got to the corner of Limnos Street and turned right for the church. Huge crowds, cars, a terrible squeeze! You just couldn't go on. We stopped and waited quite a ways from the church.

At some point the priest must've called, "Come and receive the Light." We didn't hear it, but we saw the crowd pushing and shoving, and presently candles were being lit one after the other. Car windows were half-rolled down, and those sitting inside lit their candles from the candles of those walking in the street. Mother of God, the Holy Light inside a car! Is that too where they'll sit waiting to hear the priest announce that Christ is risen?

Yes sir, that's exactly where they sat and heard the "Christ is risen." They had their car radios on, and suddenly, as if they'd prearranged it, they all started their car engines at once. They made a terrible racket. They were shouting, even swearing (and on such a day!) at those preventing them from reversing and driving off. The two old people next to us must've known from previous years, 'cause they said, "They've already got to 'Christ is risen' at the Cathedral; they're late at our church."

So these people in the cars heard the "Christ is risen" canticle on the radio, and they're going away now. In the din the cars made we could barely hear the bells ringing joyfully. But we heard the firecrackers. We kissed each other, said, "Christ is risen" and "He is risen indeed" and went home taking care so that our candles didn't blow out.

The old woman next door was waiting at the entrance with a candle to have the Holy Light from us. Father made a cross with the candle smoke on Stavro's lintel, since we weren't in our own house. Mother singed the tips of my braids for the Holy Light to "enlighten" me and then lit the lamp before the icons.

We sat at the table and cracked our eggs. We ate in silence, as if each one of us were deep in his own thoughts. Our dinner was depressing. We were alone in a strange place, a strange house. I hadn't thought of that during the sad days of Holy Week, but today, now that it was time to rejoice... My tears were dropping into the soup. I didn't want to raise my hand and wipe them, in case my mother saw me and started crying too; that wouldn't be right on such a day. I got over it after a while. I decided to say something to break the silence.

"But, Father, fancy these people receiving the Holy Light inside their cars and hearing the 'Christ is risen' inside their cars too. What do you think of that?"

I got no response. Finally our *mayeritsa* was nothing more than plain old chicken soup, but I didn't say so. Anyway, what did it matter? After the long fast it was more than all right.

Yet the folks on Symi will be eating real *mayeritsa* now. They'll have gathered at Thareini's, or Michalio's, or at Hamiotissa's, or Vassili's. They'll all be together with kith and kin, as they say, with their children and grandchildren. And the *mayeritsa* will have been cooked in the big pot, and tomorrow they'll be roasting their lamb on the spit.

We put our boiled chicken in a pan with potatoes and took it to the baker's for roasting. There were more chickens with potatoes for roasting at the bakery. Quite a few people weren't having lamb, it seems. But there

217

was lamb too: whole lambs in large baking dishes, half a lamb or leg of lamb with potatoes. Each family according to what they could afford.

We may not've had lamb for our Easter dinner, but we had salted sardines, radishes, and wine. Father says there can be no real Easter dinner without salted sardines and radishes. We cracked Easter eggs again and enjoyed our dinner.

And so our Athens Easter was over. Our first and last Athens Easter, I hope. I don't know, but it seemed a rather rushed affair to me. They don't look as though they enjoy Easter here. Again, maybe it was *us* who didn't enjoy it being in a strange place. Maybe Maria, who was with her daughters and grandchildren, enjoyed herself. Yes, but if she'd been with her daughter and grandchildren *and* on Symi too, she'd have enjoyed it even more, I'm sure.

Well, how shall I say, here in Athens you find everything ready-made. On Symi you help in getting things done: you decorate the *Epitaphios* of your parish to make it look better than that of the neighbouring parish, you chant along with the cantors, you join the others in splitting open the lamb's intestines in order to clean them, you whitewash the yard in front of the church with the other kids; in short everyone does his bit for Easter.

School's started again. We wrote an essay on "How I spent Easter." I wrote a whole lot of lies, that we spent it with friends and relatives, that we roasted a lamb and such. Everyone wrote the same stuff. I mean no-one said they'd spent Easter Sunday alone with their parents. Were there others who lied, I wonder, or was I the only girl in class, and maybe in the whole school, who was lonely?

One day some girls made up a teasing verse for me:

> *Asteria, ah, Asteria,*
> *you're such a little lady-ah!*

I beat them up. I simply lost my temper. I was sitting in a corner eating my bread ring, and they kept going on and on, *Asteria, ah Asteria...* At first I pretended not to take the bait, but then, I'm only human after all, I grabbed them by the hair and brought them down, the both of them. I'm very good at this special hold that my cousin Dino's taught me.

The tattletales went to teacher. Miss called me to the presence, and I let her have it. I wouldn't have spoken if it weren't for this incident. I'd have been patient, as there's little time left, one month, till school closes. Next year maybe I'll have a different teacher. But this time I couldn't hold my tongue any longer, and it all came out. My mother's quite right when she calls me "sharp-tongued".

"They called me Asteria," I told Miss, "and I got mad.

My name's neither Asteria nor Urania, my name's *Astradeni*! Even Father Lemonis, who's a Christian with a capital 'C', calls his own godchild Astradeni. And my name's Astradeni too, and from now on I shan't listen to whoever calls me by any other name!" That was meant for her ladyship, of course, who kept on calling me Urania all the time.

She was furious, of course. She called me impudent, cheeky and such, and took me to the Headmaster. There was another row there. The Head asked me my baptismal name, and I told him. He checked the paper I'd brought from Symi which said "Asterope". He told Miss to call me Asterope. Not that I minded really. Asterope was just fine, but I thought to myself, "Astradeni, you either make them call you Astradeni here and now, or you're not worth your salt." So I told the Head that all the Yanni's are baptised Ioannis, but who ever calls them so? Everyone calls them Yanni.

The Head laughed and said, "All right then, you win. Let's not waste our time over a name. Astradeni it shall be."

Miss was fit to burst. I didn't dare look at her. She called me Urania a few times after that. I thought maybe it was because she'd got used to it, but I didn't respond. I made as if she were addressing someone else. Pretty soon she started calling me Astradeni, and I enjoyed it tremendously. Yes sir, it felt like cool water going pleasantly down my throat.

On Saturday the 25th of May we're going on an excursion. We're going to Brauron. I kept mispronouncing the name of the place, but got it right in the end, BRAU-RON.

I wonder why we're going there; is it such an important place? I've never even heard of it. Katerina said excursions have to be to nearby places, so we can be back home by midday. Last year they'd gone to Cape Sounion. I asked her if it was beautiful, Brauron, but she didn't know. Well, we'll see.

On Symi we usually went on an excursion to Pedi. We went on foot, of course. We took along bread and cheese, an egg and some olives, and we ate our picnic lunch under the olive trees. We played games, ran, threw stones in the sea and so on. It was good fun. But I've never been on such a big excursion as this one to Brauron, and I'm looking forward to it.

Miss said Kanellopoulou's mother's coming with us, because she's an archaeologist and can explain what we're going to see. That's good, 'cause if Petropoulou was to read another report of hers copied from the encyclopaedia, I'd scream!

The suspense is unbearable! I woke up at five and walked on tiptoe to look at the clock. I did this three times. Time seems to have stood still.

We're going at nine o'clock. Last night my mother cooked a hard-boiled egg for me and made a cheese sandwich. She put the egg, the sandwich, and two apples in a plastic bag from the supermarket and I added a couple of paper napkins.

I got to school at eight. The classes that aren't going on the excursion lined up and marched to their classrooms. I sat on a step and waited. Let's see, I thought to myself, who's going to arrive first.

From the classrooms I can hear the lessons going on. It's warm and the windows are open. I can hear the first-year kids spelling in a sing-song. The first to arrive is a boy from the sixth. The sixth year is going with us. Four classes are going, the two sections of the sixth and the two sections of the fifth. The sixth-year boy is carrying a football in a net. Our friend's counting on a football game then. More kids start arriving. They've all come early, so eager are they to go on the excursion. At half past eight it's so loud in the yard, that Miss Kalliroe of the second year comes out and asks us to be quiet. But nobody listens to her, so Miss Kalliroe shuts the windows.

Then Kanellopoulou and her mother arrive. The mother's an attractive lady, a little like Mrs. Sakoulas. She's wearing a skirt and blouse and flat shoes. We get on the bus. The driver switches on the radio at once. The sound is earsplitting. It's songs by various popular singers. Not that I know them, but a girl's voice keeps saying, "And now Yanni Poulopoulos will sing GO," and such like. After the fourth song Miss asks the driver to turn the radio off. He says, "Madam", yes, he actually calls her madam! "Madam, we're going on an excursion, not to a funeral."

Miss says she will "report him." He says, "Leave us alone, lady." Miss says, "Stop the bus at once!" The driver says, "Lady, you're hard to please," and turns the radio off.

Then the kids start singing nursery rhymes at the top of their voices. The driver keeps blowing his horn in time to the singing, and Miss puffs and pants and fans herself. I love all this. There's a terrible din and Miss is miserable. I just love it!

I'm sitting at the very back of the bus. The seats up front are always taken by others who save them for their friends. I'm sitting alone, with my picnic bag on the seat next to me. We go uphill. You can see all of Athens below: houses, houses everywhere and not a spot of green anywhere.

It took an hour to get to Brauron. Still, we made very good time, says the driver. And he's right, 'cause the other buses haven't got here yet. We get off the bus taking our picnic bags with us. We're not all of us carrying plastic bags. Some have these bags they call rucksacks. They're very nice and have pockets on the outside too. George Sakinos has got a bag like that.

Miss takes us to a field and asks us to sit there till the others arrive. And we must by no means go down to the main road. The morning's still chilly. There's dew on

223

the grass. And there are so many of the edible weeds growing everywhere. My mother would've been delighted. And there's that aromatic root that makes the whole house smell sweet if you put it in with boiling greens. And there's camomile and poppies too.

It occurs to me that spring's almost over. It's come and gone, and I've hardly noticed. How should I have noticed when I didn't see any grass grow, any poppies, any swallows? Come to think of it, I haven't seen one single swallow in Kypseli. Can it be there aren't any swallows in Athens? No, there's two flying together right now. But it seems swallows don't come to Kypseli, and quite right too. Where would they built a nest, and what with? Where would they find earth to mould into mud-balls for their nest? What would they line it with to make it soft for laying their eggs? Where would they find hair and feathers, and what would they feed their young with? Are there any worms and flies in Athens? Well, as far as flies go, there's plenty. Yes, somehow, Athens doesn't seem right for swallows. But then maybe it's me who didn't see them. Maybe there are swallows in Athens, it's just that I haven't been looking for them.

And here, sure these must be daffodils; it's the right season for them. Saint Constantine's will smell wonderful now. The whole hillside down to Kalyvato'll be yellow with daffodils, to say nothing of the smell that makes you quite faint. It was my late Uncle Vassili who planted those flowers. He was my mother's brother, but I never knew him as he died young, at sixteen. He didn't die exactly, he drowned.

He was their eldest, their first-born. Grandma Eleni never got over it. In her last days she would start talking to him as if he were sitting beside her. At such times I had a weird feeling.

He was just sixteen at the time. The girls, my mother and her sisters, were younger. My mother was only ten. Vassili was a shepherd. He left with the flock at dawn and came back in the evening. He usually went to the pond at Glyfonies to let the flock drink.

One day in Spring they brought him to Grandma drowned. Mother says the water was still dripping from his clothes. They said he was looking at himself in the water straightening the part in his hair, and he got dizzy and fell in and drowned. Not that the pond's very deep. The water's hardly two metres deep. Nor is it a real pond. The shepherds made it to water their flocks. They dug a big hole and strengthened its sides with stones. In the summer, when the water level's low, you can see the stones round the sides. So the boy got a dizzy spell and drowned. Some say he quarrelled with a friend who pushed him in. The case was even taken to court. But it didn't seem the other fellow was to blame. The fact is the boy drowned at sixteen.

As the years passed, the daffodils multiplied and spread everywhere. My mother thinks of Vassili all the year round. She burns incense for him, and his picture's among the icons with the photos of all our other dead. She has memorial prayers read for him and makes *kollyva*. But in the spring, she says, he's before her at every step when she looks at his daffodils. And she always picked daffodils to place on his grave at Saint Constantine's where he's buried together with my grandma, Grandpa Sotiri, Aunt Dikissi, Great-Grandma Martha, and the monks.

"Are you looking at the narcissi?" Mrs. Kanellopoulou asks me.

"On Symi we call them daffodils," I tell her.

"Ah, you must be Astradeni." So she knows who I am. Her daughter must've told her about me. "We two have something in common." I wonder how she and I can have something in common. "We both have ancient names. My name's Haricleia."

"Ever so pleased to meet you," I say, and she laughs; not mockingly, of course, but she laughs just the same. I blush. I always say the wrong thing. What was the proper thing to've said, I wonder? She apparently understood and stroked my head.

The other buses arrive. The Head, who's come with us, whistles for us to gather together. We stand in line to go through a gate. It's very muddy underfoot. If you aren't careful, you may get stuck in the mud, to say nothing of your shoes getting covered with mud all over anyway. Kanellopoulou's mother climbs on a rock, so we can all see and hear her. She starts speaking in a pleasant, calm voice. She doesn't rush; she talks slowly and clearly.

She tells us that Brauron is one of the oldest places in Attica and that the goddess Diana was worshipped here. Then she asks us whether we remember Iphigenia, and we all shout, "Yeees!" Then she tells us that Iphigenia, who was kidnapped by Diana when her father Agamemnon was about to sacrifice her, had lived here at Brauron and had brought with her from a faraway place

226

the ancient wooden statue of the goddess.

Then she takes us to see Iphigenia's tomb. We walk past some rocks and come to a place like a cave. It's very stuffy in there. The rock is low over our heads, and there's a lot of damp. So that's the tomb of Iphigenia. Fancy. These things you take to be fairy tales did actually happen. Since there's a tomb, there was an Iphigenia. And since there was an Iphigenia, there must've been a goddess Diana, and that means... but I'm getting muddled.

We come out on to a flat area. It's paved with marble slabs and has columns all around. Kanellopoulou's mother goes ahead and climbs on a round stone. She starts telling us about a feast that was held every five years and was called "the Brauronia". She says they brought little girls here aged seven to eleven, and left them here to be young priestesses till the time came for them to get married. On the day of the feast they wore yellow tunics and danced a special dance.

"And did the girls live here alone?" asks one of the kids.

"Yes, with the older priestesses," says Mrs. Kanellopoulou.

I was afraid to go down below. But the three women stood in the door and waited. I was scared, but went down. I lifted my tunic so it wouldn't get soiled and went down. But the chapel wasn't black with the soot from the fire. It was all white and had beautiful marble columns. And where the altar is in the Holy of Holies, there was a marble table without a cloth but only a big censer on it.

"And in this place we found their little rooms," says Mrs. Kanellopoulou. "For the ceremony they wore a beautiful yellow tunic, and they were called *arctoi,* little bears, that is."

Then the three women stood before the marble table. They dropped something in the censer that made a hissing noise. They raised their arms high and started saying incomprehensible things. I couldn't understand what they were saying. I could only make out a few words: Diana, bear, virgin, sacrifice.

My feet seem rooted to the ground. They feel heavy and cold. Fear makes my tongue stick to the roof of my mouth, and my heart's beating to bursting point. I hold my picnic bag tight with all my strength. The *dream,* the dream I'd had my first night in Athens! The same talk, the same words. How come? How can these things happen? I'd never heard of these things before, so how could I have the dream? What can it all mean?

The kids have walked on, and Mrs. Kanellopoulou's telling them something else. I can see them all gathered around her but can't hear what's being said, and I feel alone and scared. I run up to them. I wish we'd leave this place at once. I wish we'd go home.

I don't remember what else we saw, what else we were told. The dream was pestering my mind. Who should I tell about it? Mrs. Kanellopoulou maybe? Never! She's a stranger, she'll think I'm crazy. But how come I had the dream?

It feels like time has stopped. The others are eating their picnics, playing football. I'm sitting on the grass dumbfounded. Why did this thing happen to me? My head feels as if it's going to burst.

We get into the buses at last, and it's already after-noon when we get home. In my bag the food's un-touched. Should I tell Mother or shouldn't I? And what's she to make of sacrifices and bears? I guess I'd better try and make sense of it all by myself. Perhaps I should forget about it and decide it hasn't happened. But that's out of the question; I keep thinking about it all the time.

At home I ring the bell, but no-one comes to the door. I ring again, nothing. Where can Mother've gone? She never goes out. Maybe she's gone to the bakery, which means she'll be back any minute now. I hope so, 'cause I'm so tired and so giddy.

I'm standing by the main entrance when Mr. Aleko ar-rives. He opens the door with his key, and I go in with him. Mr. Aleko goes into his flat, and I sit outside our door. What on earth is Mother doing? I'm uneasy anyway, and I don't like the dark in the passage. I switch the light on. Mr. Aleko opens his door.

"What are you doing out there alone?" he asks. "Is your Mother out?"

"Yes," I nod.

"Come in and sit down till she comes back," he says.

On another occasion I'd 've found an excuse in order not to accept his invitation. But now I just go in. Not that these people have ever done anything to me, but I don't much care for them. In the hall there's a couch, a small table and the TV. I sit and wait. Mother must come back any minute now.

Mr. Aleko's lit a cigarette and gone into the kitchen. I can see a fridge, a rubbish bin, an alarm clock on the fridge. His wife must be out.

"Won't you come in here and keep me company while I'm cooking?" I hear him calling to me.

I don't want to. Mother's taking too long; she should've been back by now. It's out of the question that she's taking so long at the bakery. Maybe she's gone up to the roof? She sometimes likes going up there to look at the mountains in the distance. She doesn't see the blocks of flats, the laundry hanging on the roof terraces, the TV aerials; she only sees the mountains. And, of course, she remembers Symi. She imagines she's on Symi.

"I'm going to look and see if my mother's back," I say. Mr. Aleko comes out of the kitchen. I don't like the way he's looking at me.

"Where d'you want to go, ducky?" he says. I'm scared, I don't like it. I want to get out of here this minute.

"I want to go right now!" I shout.

"Come here, you silly girl," he says and grabs me as if I were as light as a feather. He puts one arm round my waist and his free hand over my mouth. He drags me into the kitchen. Music is playing softly on the radio. With a sudden gesture he turns the volume on high.

I'm shaking with anger and fear.

"You beast!" I growl and give him a punch. But I can't shout, I'm unable to shout! I keep hitting him with my picnic bag. The egg is smashed, and eggwhite and yolk are scattered all over. The apple is crushed. I hit him on the head over and over again with all the might of my fury. I know what he wants to do to me, I sense it. I kick him in the shin, and he gets mighty angry. He says he's dealt with many of the likes of me before.

His hand over my mouth's almost blocking my nostrils too. I'm going to kill him, I *want* to kill him. I want to see him squashed into a pulp. *The dream!* Is *that* what the dream was about, that sacrifice? But why, who for?

No, not my dress. Don't lift my dress. No, not my dress, my tunic. No, no, not my tunic — not my tunic, no!

EUGENIA FAKINOU

Eugenia Fakinou was born in Alexandria in 1945. She studied graphic arts in Athens and completed a course as a tourist guide. In 1976 she founded the popular puppet theatre "Tin Town".

Eugenia Fakinou has written and illustrated a great number of children's books. Her first novel, *Astradeni*, was published in 1982 and immediately became a bestseller. She has since published four more novels, *The Seventh Garment, The Big Blue Sea, Cool Cat,* and *Sugar on the Edge.* Her books have been translated into German, English, French and Hungarian.

H. E. CRITON

H.E. Criton studied English and Comparative Literature at Yale University and has taught English Language and Literature in Greece, England and Germany. He is a contributor to literary periodicals in Athens as a critic of fiction.

WHAT DOES MRS. FREEMAN WANT,

Petros Abatzoglou

Here is the portrait of an extraordinary – yet in many ways typical – English couple, as seen through the eyes of a fascinated, ouzo-guzzling Greek narrator, reminiscing on a sun-drenched beach. Under his passionate, yet humorous, scrutiny, Mrs. Freeman and her husband come alive with great vividness, while retaining intact the mystery of their "otherness." The book is much more than the story of Mrs. Freeman's life and times; it also offers an ironical insight into the confrontation of two cultures, two different ways of looking at the world.

FOOL'S GOLD

Maro Douka

"My father, thunderstruck, was demanding to know: but when? This is madness! Impossible. When at last he replaces the receiver in a grand Shakespearean manner – my father has it in the blood – he broke the news to us: Dictatorship. My mother cried out and collapsed in a heap on the sofa. Calliope the maid, as part of her duties, always manages to sense the right moment for a restorative coffee, and set off for the kitchen. My father repeated: Dictatorship, do you hear! I stared at him, shaking off sleep."

This is how Myrsini Panayotou, an Athenian girl about to

234

start university, learns of the coup d'état that brought to power the infamous dictatorship of the "Colonels" in her country in the early hours of Friday, 21st April 1967. The child of a well-to-do family, Myrsini enthusiastically joins the underground resistance, making common cause with a varied cast of characters from backgrounds very different from her own. After an early failed love affair she gets engaged to George, a political prisoner, only to find her human instincts increasingly difficult to reconcile with her idealistic philosophy once he is released. The story moves towards its climax as Myrsini becomes involved in the bloody events of 17th November 1973, when tanks were used to evict students from the Athens Polytechnic. At the same time the fortunes of Myrsini's family form a backdrop at once touching and bizarre to an impressionable girl's unflinching search for a true identity, both for herself and for her country.

Fool's Gold is a sparkling first novel by a talented writer, one of the foremost of a new generation which grew up under the shadow of the events Maro Douka describes.

THE BUILDERS

Giorgos Heimonas

Giorgos Heimonas was born at Kavala in 1939. He studied psychiatry at the University of Athens and the University of Paris, and he lives in Athens, where he works as a professor, physician, and author. His mysterious and moving narratives have made him one of Greece's most renowned contemporary writers.

To enter into a Heimonas text is not so much to read the written word as to experience it. His characters repeatedly suggest that the word of their experience flows through the body toward the lips but never reaches speech. Accordingly, Heimonas creates a metamorphosed language and a genre which are

235

neither poetry nor fiction in a conventional sense yet share certain qualities of each. In *The Builders* the protagonist is the herald of a new order of speech and feeling. The text suggests that we cease, as it were, to listen to experience with our neighbour's ear; rather we should feel the world through a sort of language of the nerves. Thus, the narrative does not articulate an idea or situation so much as pulse with sensations of pain, joy, discovery. The feeling of existence becomes its meaning. In Heimonas' words, the world becomes an image and humanity itself the message.

JAGUAR

Alexandros Kotzias

The author has called *The Jaguar* "an extravagant story." He employs an extravagant style to stress the irony of his heroine's attempt to preserve a false image of her moral superiority in the process of promoting selfish ends.

The historical events referred to in Dimitra's account of herself and her family belong to the Second World War period. Dimitra, a mathematics teacher, had been an active member of the leftist resistance movement during the Nazi occupation of Greece and was persecuted as a communist in the civil war era that followed. Years later, she likes to think of herself as an uncompromising individual engaged in a noble struggle to promote the ideals of a socialist revolution.

The unexpected return of her sister-in-law Philio from America to claim an inheritance forces her to take a good look at the past. Her breathless interior monologue throughout the night of her confrontation with Philio reveals Dimitra's obstinate refusal to accept the "bourgeois" compromises she has meanwhile made and has been comfortably living with for the past ten years.

The extravagant melodrama of Dimitra's rhetoric often

becomes a caricature of dialectic reasoning, a comic version of double-think paring reality to make it fit within the confines of wishful thinking and self-righteousness. When the verbal torrent is finally spent, the comedy fades leaving a bitter aftertaste of the pathos of self-deception.

In native South American religion the jaguar was regarded as a fierce deity representing forces of war, destruction and human sacrifice.

KOULA

Menis Koumandareas

A "brief encounter" on the Athenian Underground brings together two people, Koula and Dimitris, from entirely different backgrounds and ages. For a few weeks they manage to break loose from their respective shackles and meet in a kind of no man's land of passionate discovery. The couple's emotional fluctuations are charted with remarkable precision and subtlety, in a low-key tone that fully captures the muted drama of their meeting and parting.

FAREWELL ANATOLIA

Dido Sotiriou

Farewell Anatolia is a tale of paradise lost and of shattered innocence; a tragic fresco of the fall of Hellenism in Asia Minor; a stinging indictment of Great Power politics, oil-lust and corruption.

Dido Soteriou's novel – a perennial best-seller in Greece

since it first appeared in 1962 — tells the story of Manolis Axiotis, a poor but resourceful villager born near the ancient ruins of Ephesus. Axiotis is a fictional protagonist and eyewitness to an authentic nightmare: Greece's ''Asia Minor Catastrophe,'' the death or expulsion of two million Greeks from Turkey by Kemal Attaturk's revolutionary forces in the late summer of 1922.

Manolis Axiotis' chronicle of personal fortitude, betrayed hope, and defeat resonates with the greater tragedy of two nations: Greece, vanquished and humiliated; Turkey, bloodily victorious. Two neighbours linked by bonds of culture and history yet diminished by mutual greed, cruelty and bloodshed.

Farewell Anatolia has been translated into French, Russian, Hungarian. A Turkish translation appeared in 1970, and was hailed as a major contribution to reconciliation between the two neighbours.

ACHILLES' FIANCÉE

Alki Zei

The scene is Paris, sometime after the 1967 military *coup* in Greece. Eleni, together with a group of her friends and fellow political exiles, finds herself working as an extra in a French film: *The Horror Train.* It is not the first time Eleni has been caught up in a deadly drama, nor is it her first ride on a ''horror train''. As the director waves his arms, shouting directions and re-shooting the sequence, Eleni's mind wanders to her first train ride:

''Athens-Piraeus. My first big trip by train.
— You're Eleni? I'm Achilles.
They don't ask which Achilles. One name is enough ...''

For the rest of her life, Eleni will be ''Achilles' Fiancée,'' fiancée of the guerilla leader, the brave, handsome *kapetanios* whose code-name is Achilles. In the demonstrations against the German occupiers of Greece, in prison where she waits for a death sentence during the post-war persecution of suspected leftists, in exile in Tashkent where the exiled Greek communists fight amongst themselves, and finally in Paris, she will always be known as "Achilles' Fiancée." But somewhere along the way Eleni becomes an independent character with a mind of her own. As she begins to doubt the slogans that she fought for when she was a blind follower of leaders like her fiancé, Eleni involves us in her own private world of self-discovery. It is a woman's world, where human warmth and deep friendships matter more than abstract ideals, where young girls fall in love and enjoy wearing pretty clothes.

The Greek word for a novel is *mythistorema,* a word that combines "myth" and "history." In her story of a young woman's struggle to survive through an extraordinary period of Greek history, Alki Zei has woven the threads of her own quasi-mythical life into the stuff of history. The result is a compelling and beautiful novel that opens a new window on modern Greek history.